Troll Gurl

and the Cursed Kingdom

Other Books by Jennifer Friess

*The Wind Could Blow a Bug*

*When You Least Expect It*

*Be Careful What You Wish For*

# Troll Gurl
# and the Cursed Kingdom

By Jennifer Friess

Mr. Ugly-Man Entertainment
Adrian, Michigan

Mr. Ugly-Man Entertainment
Adrian, Michigan
First Edition December 2016
Text copyright ©2016 by Jennifer Friess
All Rights Reserved, including the right of reproduction in whole or in part in any form.
To book an event or to purchase additional copies, please visit:
imnotstalkingyou.com


ISBN 9780692820544

*To all the assholes who always made me feel like I wasn't anything. Here is the proof that you were fuckin' wrong.*

*Let my hate on these pages consume you.*

# GEEKDOM

It crawls under my skin
It bubbles & churns
tending to collect in
stomach and rot & gnaw & char
leaving me weak at times
when I  need to be the strongest
reminding me

There are lesser people
they might walk & talk
and seem smart
but they are disabled inside
socially impaired
abnormally interacted
grotesquely under-de-somethingized.

Cry, pray, cut, hit, ache
for
It to leave you
But it coats your soul
It shadows your thoughts
clouds your memories

It makes you shiver when you wake up in the dark of night,
revolted to be inside your own body.

"I am very sorry to tell you,
Mr. & Mrs. Doe
what we thought was a healthy girl
just minutes ago
Is a geek in human clothing
We'll understand
If you want to go
But take the geek with you
We don't care for those."

**L**ong ago, in a time before we confined our magic to fiber optic cables and microchips, there was a beautiful kingdom nestled in a valley, surrounded by mountains. The ebony mountains only brightened when the sun shone directly upon them, the peaks frosted with snow nine months out of the year. Rolling hills led up to the mountains, carpeted in thick, green grass on which white cows with black spots grazed. The fields of grain and beans created a patchwork in the countryside. In between the patchwork fields were modest wooden cabins that housed families, smoke from the fireplaces curling up towards the sky, the scent of the burned wood ingraining itself with the scent of the cows and dewy grass.

To the north stood a stone castle where the king for the whole valley lived. It wasn't as large as the castles on the other side of the mountains, but that was fine. Everyone knows what they say about kings with big castles; they must be compensating for their small family jewels.

The people of the kingdom of Inniskellin were happy, for the most part. Sure, there was the occasional brawl at the pub or a land dispute. But everyone got up at the crack of dawn, worked hard, and slept well at night. Inniskellin was growing, little by little, every year.

King Talbot was not the brightest king that had ever existed. But he wasn't particularly cruel either, so the villagers let his reign continue with no motion to remove him from the throne. He was young, still only twenty when his father died unexpectedly and he took over the ruling duties. That was going on five years ago.

King Talbot was single and a ladies man. He always had a beautiful woman on his arm. At royal balls, his dance card was perpetually full. Coming to power as he entered adulthood may have contributed to his hard-partying ways. He had dark hair and rather plain looks while being slightly overweight and not particularly athletic. But the lasses were all over him, because they all dreamed of one day becoming queen. And the king liked it that way.

The people who lived in the villages directly around the castle were known as living "in the shadow of the castle." They perceived themselves to be better than the rest of the villages in Inniskellin, because they saw the king more frequently as he traveled in and out of the castle. This caused the people of those close villages to put on airs. The faraway villagers thought of them as snooty for assigning themselves an honor that really only existed in their big heads. Even those within the castle walls did not like the villages in the shadow of the castle, although the king loved the attention they showered upon him.

One day, he was at a faire in a village in the shadow of the castle. All the beautiful ladies were hanging on him, trying to get a dance as the band played a raucous tune. An older woman with a long nose and crooked, umber teeth wearing ragged clothes approached him.

"May I have a dance, sonny?" she screeched.

"Oh, definitely not" those who were witness say he replied.

"What? Well, why not? I just want some face time with my king," she responded.

"No. What you need is a new face!" the king yelled too loudly to his hangers-on. He guffawed, his belly bouncing with the exertion. He was eating too many treats baked for him by the wannabee queens, and it was showing.

"Excuse me?" the old woman replied in disbelief.

"Wow. Not only is she ugly, she is deaf and dumb too!"

More laughter erupted.

"My ears better be deceiving me. I would hate to have to punish you for disrespecting an old woman."

"Oh, right, like you could punish me. My royal guards would have you subdued in no time. And I wonder if you even *are* a woman anymore. You are probably all shrunken, like a dried fruit," the king snickered. The crowd doting on him hooted and hollered their agreement.

"You best find some respect for your citizens fast, or they will all pay for what you have done here today."

"No one can harm me. I am the king! Now get out of my sight, you ugly old witch." The king even made a gesture with his hands, as if he were sweeping her away and out of his sight.

"Oh, you have no idea how right you are, sonny!" The unknown woman cackled loudly. She raised her arms to the sky and magenta smoke began to billow around her.

"I am a witch! And I don't appreciate being talked to that way. And neither do these greedy whores around you, but they won't tell you that. You think that your precious guards can protect you from a curse? I think not. I will spread a curse across your land. Death will surround you. As the years pass, it will only get worse, until your whole kingdom and everything in it shall perish."

Half the people gathered chuckled, thinking this was a joke or an illusion, including the king. The other half trembled in their boots, knowing this could be the end of the pretty charmed existence they had enjoyed up until now.

"But I feel sorry for your kingdom, all those who will die innocently because of your incivility. So, I will give you the key to breaking the curse. Your first born son must kiss the girl in the land who has the truest beauty, through and through. You better hope that he is blessed with the gift of knowing true beauty that you yourself lack."

And she cackled, disappearing into her purple cloud, and was gone.

All the villagers stared at the king, waiting to see his reaction. They looked to him to know how to respond to this horrific event.

And he laughed.

The king laughed off the curse.

A few others did too. They were suck-ups who would agree with the king on anything. If he said the sky was green, they would agree with him.

The others simply looked at one another. And when their eyes met each other's, they all reflected the same uncertainty. And this spread like wildfire as they told what had happened between the king and the witch, over and over again, to their families, friends, neighbors, and acquaintances.

At the same instant the angry witch's curse spread across the land, a baby girl was born. The parents were horrified. The newborn came out as the ugliest baby they had ever seen. When the baby was placed in the mother's arms, the mother screamed. The mother was so revolted by her baby's appearance that she opened her arms and the infant fell to the floor hard, and began to cry. Not wanting to kill it, but also not wanting to keep the child, the midwife took it to an orphanage in the next village. It was run by a lady named Miss Peters. She accepted the deformed, mutant-looking pale infant. The baby girl had a giant, bulbous nose. One eyelid drooped lower over the right eye than the left. Her eyes did not contain a bright circle of color, but rather a milky glaze that hid whatever true color may lay behind it. She would tell the girl that she had been found on the doorstep with no one around, to prevent her from ever hoping to reunite with her parents who would never accept her. Miss Peters gave her a beautiful name, hoping it would make up some for her gruesome appearance. She prayed it would improve with age. She named her Guinevere, the name of legend, and often understood to mean "white phantom."

T hey all felt the same worry that had not before hung over Inniskellin. Generations of villagers had experienced good fortune. There was still the divide between the rich and the poor. But the people had enough to eat, they were all happy and healthy. No war had come to them. But they could all feel the shift now. As the days passed, an anxiety permeated them as they had never experienced before. It hung on their clothes like campfire smoke. They always were just a little on edge. It was as though a gloomy cloud hung over each of their heads, even though the sun still shined.

But they began to notice subtle changes. The leaves of all the plants started to always be black on the tips. The fruit and vegetables were still grown and harvested. But it made everyone nervous. The cattle stopped getting quite as fat as they used to. Some chalked it up to the people's paranoia. But when weighed year to year at market, the numbers proved their suspicions right.

In other noteworthy news, shortly after the witch's curse, King Talbot abruptly married. Some said that he had to.

Seven months later, all the mysterious happenings were momentarily forgotten with the birth of the prince. The bouncing baby boy was chubby and beautiful, with eyes like molasses and curls to match.

The girl named Guinevere grew to be obedient and hard-working, helping Miss Peters with the chores whilst the other children played. Early on they would invite Ginny to play with them, only to be cruel to her. A girl with long, golden hair named Lydia was always the ring leader. She had been at the orphanage since she was a toddler, and was roughly the same age as Ginny. She would have been pretty, had her face not wore a pinched expression at all times as if she smelled something rotten.

The other orphans would play hide-and-seek with her, then forget to seek her, heading off to play another game that did not include her. Sometimes the girls would play knights and robbers and make Ginny be a robber, so that they could tie her up. Once they bound her to a tree in the woods and left her there. Miss Peters did not come looking for Ginny till morning, commenting that she herself was too afraid of the dark to enter the forest at night. Ginny would continue to have nightmares about that incident in the woods for the rest of her life.

Miss Peters told Ginny, "Do not let anyone see that you are weak. Do not let them see that they hurt you. Do not let them see you cry. They will exploit it until you are completely broken." Ginny felt that Miss Peters should make the other girls stop their behavior. But Miss Peters's words had told her that it was Ginny's burden to bear. Ginny was the one who needed to change, not the other girls. She needed to grow a tougher skin against all the teasing and torture. But Ginny could not find that inner strength inside. She always broke down. And that was when the others would tear her apart.

Once a fellow orphan girl named Bridget, who was very fair but so dim she sometimes forgot her own name, happened to touch Ginny's hair during a game of tag. It was not hard to catch Ginny, as her extra-large feet and short legs gave her a speed and agility disadvantage. It was probably the only reason they let her join in at all. She was always the first one out.

"Your hair is soft," Bridget remarked in surprise.

"Why wouldn't it be?"

"I just assumed it would be nasty and stiff like the cow's hide." It did not escape Ginny's cloudy vision that Bridget always escaped milking duties. Or that Bridget was comparing her to a cow's ass.

"I wash it with the same soap as you do yours. You assumed it would be unpleasant because I am ugly?" Ginny meant for it to come out incredulous, but instead her words were feeble.

"Of course." Satisfied that their non-conversation was over and Ginny was safely eliminated, Bridget ran back to the game with her band of make-shift sisters.

Ginny knew that is how they all thought of each other. And even at this young age, she knew that that sorority would never include her. She always thought that they teased her all the time only because she looked different. But Bridget's comment had upset her more than usual. Ginny now knew that they didn't just think she was different on the outside, they thought she was on the inside as well. She had hoped she would one day grow to be more beautiful and they would accept her. But this new development made Ginny lose all but the tiniest hope of that happening. They made up a jump rope chant, in her honor, that they sang over and over again all day long as each girl took their turn:

I smell the roses
I jump with my feet
All that is beautiful
Can't be beat
I see a monster
The troll gurl
Watch out!
She will eat you
faster, faster
You better watch out
She'll eat me too.

After Miss Peters turned down the lanterns and ordered all the orphans to silence and sleep, she always returned to her nearby cabin with the thatch-covered roof for the duration of the night. The girls would then prattle on endlessly about one silly topic or another, sometimes for hours, until exhaustion finally overtook them. Ginny did much of the work that had to be done on the farm and in the kitchen as the others chose not to. She was always exhausted when she hit her pillow, and wished they would all be quiet and go to sleep. But she had to stay awake until the last one was unconscious. She had learned her lesson the hard way. Many nights they had gotten together, coordinated and executed tactile assaults on her while she was in slumber.

Tonight they were supposing on the existence of magic.

"I think magic is real. It has to be," Marta declared, always the dreamer.

Ginny often had strong opinions on these topics, but she knew better than to speak up. Last time that happened they had cut all her hair off. It was only just now growing out.

"Real things are rain and mud and cow shit—all the things we are surrounded by every day in this hellhole," Lydia sneered into the darkness.

"So Lydia, you don't believe that if you kiss enough frogs, one will turn into a prince?" Natalie asked.

"Never."

"But what about this curse? Without magic, there would be no curse," Angie inquired.

Although it was dark, Angie's face popped into Ginny's mind at the sound of her ragged voice. She had hair that was only one shade shy of being orange, and hung long and loose, though Angie never bothered to brush it.

"There's no curse. It is all just stories the crazy old folks tell to scare us," Lydia replied.

"No, it's real!" Angie protested.

"Oh really? Then how come we are still here? How come the kingdom hasn't disappeared like cotton candy on your tongue?"

"Now that sounds like magic," Marta whispered.

"You've never had cotton candy," Angie retorted.

"Have too." Lydia always had to have the last word. It didn't matter if it was a lie.

There was silence for a few moments.

"So you think when I wish on a falling star, it means nothing?" Marta asked.

"Nothing. Life, death. None of it means anything," Lydia responded.

"That is a horrible way to be," Marta said.

"It's real," Lydia stated.

"The king is smart. He wouldn't fight a curse by collecting more taxes and drafting more knights if no such thing existed."

"The king isn't smart at all."

Ginny could agree with that, from fragments of what she heard the adults say.

"Maybe it is all a lie. Maybe it is just a way for the prince to be the talk of the kingdom. Some day he will pick out the best kisser to be his queen."

"Nobody said that he would have to marry the girl whose kiss breaks the curse."

"But why wouldn't he?"

"Because maybe he won't love her."

"Maybe love is the real magic," Marta offered.

A hush fell over all the girls then. They were all here, stuck in the care of Miss Peters. None of them had known a mother or father's love. But the others had hope of one day marrying a dashing stranger. Ginny had no such preconceived notions. There would always be only herself, and whatever self-reliance she could muster. When all their breathing fell even in the room, she crept outside into the pitch black night to look at the sky.

Ginny could not shut her mind down. Was there really a curse? And if so, why wasn't the kingdom destroyed yet? Most of all, why had Ginny ever been born to look this way, instead of normal? She felt normal inside, she thought. How had the outside gone so wrong?

Ginny yearned to know what it was like to be beautiful. She wished one day that she would wake up and could peel the ugly off of her face. She was so tired of how everyone looked at her. They saw her glazed eyes, her droopy eyelid, her giant nose, and assumed she was also feeble-minded. But she had millions of ideas run through her head every day. Brilliant ideas! She had feelings! If you threw rocks at her, did she not hurt? If you cut her, did she not bleed? There were just as many deep thoughts going on inside her brain as anyone else. Probably more than some of the air-brained girls she was forced to share a bedroom with.

She looked up at the stars then. They seemed so bright tonight. Then she saw it: her first ever shooting star. Hadn't

Marta, so small and impressionable with her big round eyes and short black hair, said you should wish on it? So Ginny wished her deepest, most heartfelt wish. She wished to be pretty.

It might seem logical that those in a kingdom sentenced to death would want to escape such a fate. But it all began slowly enough at first that it was difficult to tell if unfortunate instances could be contributed to the curse, or just nature having a bad day. By the time the residents realized they were indeed living under a curse, so did the surrounding kingdoms. Usually traveling between the neighboring lands happened freely. But post-curse, the other kingdoms would not allow residents from Inniskellin to travel across their lands, let alone take up residence. They were trying to stop the spread of the curse, as if it were to settle upon them next. It became a criminal offense, punishable by death. If you were going to die now because you traveled, or later due to a curse, which would you choose? The residents became resigned to their fate.

"You better all stay seated back there. No funny business," Miss Peters ordered as she took the reins of the horse they borrowed from a neighbor to get to market. She was a slender woman who always wore her long gray hair pulled snuggly into a bun on the back of her head. Her eyebrows were always at a strange angle, as if her hair was so tight it was actually pulling her face back as well. And even though it was tight, there was one wisp that always escaped daily as she did the cooking or dishes or laundry for up to twenty bodies.

"But there isn't any room back here," Natalie whined, her feet surrounded by jars of fruit spread on one side and bags of potatoes on the other. She fidgeted, wearing her favorite purple dress which accented her rosacea-touched cheeks below her crown of curly, auburn locks. Angie leaned over and whispered something into her ear, and then gave a wicked smile in Ginny's direction as she was the last one to climb aboard the wooden wagon.

It was one of their few cart rides a year to the castle to trade produce. Ginny must have been around ten years old at the time.

When Ginny tried to sit down in the empty spot next to Natalie, she quickly slid over and said, "You can't sit here. There is no room."

"But there was a moment ago," Ginny said, confused.

"It is a long ride. I don't want to be crowded," Natalie replied.

Ginny just stood there.

"What are you, deaf? She said there ain't no more room," Lydia chided.

Ginny's shoulders slumped more than usual as she climbed over that bench to the next one. She was met with Angie's revolted stare.

"No room here," Angie said, shrugging.

Then Miss Peters set the horse into motion, pulling the wagon and spilling Ginny on top of the goods. The other girls laughed loudly at her. She stood back up, and managed to keep her balance while standing. That is, until the wheel bumped over a particularly large rock. Then she fell again, to even more uproarious laughter.

"What is going on back there? I told you no horsing around."

"It's not us, Miss Peters."

It was humorous that Lydia knew she would be the first one Miss Peters suspected.

"Ginny won't sit down."

"Ginny, sit. If you can't ride properly in the cart, then you will have to walk beside it," Miss Peters warned, her gray eyes piercing, the exact same shade as her hair.

Ginny just wanted to crawl somewhere and hide. Instead, she had never felt more on display as she tried to keep her footing under their penetrating glares.

It was not more than a few minutes later that she had to grab onto the side to keep from falling out. The instigators were beside themselves with delight. That was when Ginny got evicted from the wagon.

"And you better keep up!" Miss Peters barked as a threat.

While Ginny's short legs ached by the time they reached the merchant square inside the castle walls, it was much easier to walk herself than trying to stand and stay upright in the rickety cart.

There was less to take to market this year as the crops were all affected by the mysterious plant plague. No longer only blackened tips, the fruits and vegetables were smaller than they usually were. As they tended to their booth, there was suddenly a flurry of activity heading their way. Miss Peters pushed Ginny behind her, but Ginny peeked out from behind her long skirt anyway. The king and his son were touring the markets. They tried to look like it was a casual visit, but it was really to gauge the effect the plant plague was having on the food supply. It was enough to cause concern. Ginny had never seen the king before, or the prince. At the orphanage, she saw few men at all. The prince must have been close to her age. He had black, wavy hair and dark brown eyes. He seemed unsure and did not smile. It made him appear sad.

As they passed right by the booth, Ginny could not help but lean out to get a better look. Losing her balance, she knocked over two wooden crates, making a terrible racket. The king never looked or broke stride as he waved and smiled at his subjects, moving his way easily through the market. But the prince paused then, turning to approach Ginny. He smiled and offered her his hand. His smile was so bright and sweet that she didn't think before reaching out and letting him pull her up.

"You OK?" he asked, to which Ginny could only nod her oversized head in response. He nodded to her and quickly caught up with his father.

In that moment, Ginny forgot that she was not like everyone else. She was totally enchanted with the prince and how nice he had been to her. It was all quickly destroyed like a smoke ring from a pipe.

"Ew, now the prince has troll germs," Lydia sneered.

Just like that, Ginny was reminded that she had a place. That place was behind everyone else. That place was walking next to the horse cart on the way home. But she did not even try to keep up this time, even as the sun fell behind the mountains and they traveled deeper into the gloomy, old-growth forest.

Ginny continued to catch glimpses of the prince in the market in the courtyard of the castle a few times a year when they took their dwindling harvest and crafts to trade. The other orphans would scatter soon after arrival to socialize and shop. Ginny always stayed behind at the booth to help Miss Peters and wait to steal a peek at the prince.

Ginny knew the other girls stole as well, but more tangible items. At night, before the lanterns were turned out, they would compare who had brought home the best haul. It made Ginny sick. Didn't they know they were hurting the reputation of the orphanage? Of Miss Peters? Everyone assumed the orphans were thieves—why prove them right beyond a shadow of a doubt? The other girls were too self-centered to realize the more vendors they stole from, the less those same vendors would have to make a charitable donation to their quarters and meals. They were selfish and rude and despicable. They would never be friends with her.

*Ginny didn't want to be friends with them anyway.*

It was a powerful revelation, but it provided little comfort. It made the existing loneliness grow stronger still.

Ginny thought that the jig was up one day at midlight when she was thirteen years old and the royal caravan pulled up to the orphanage door. She had been in the barn feeding the animals while the others had been in the dormitory. But the thunder of twelve sets of hooves on the practically grown over passage through the woods was a rare sound and one that got all their attentions. The metal shoes made an eerie echo off the gnarled bark of the aged forest.

The regiment of royal guards flanked the carriage of the king and young prince. Some carried tall flags bearing the seal of Inniskellin, while others had large swords strapped to their hips. Ginny quickly dropped what she was doing in the barn, leaving the chickens to eat straight out of the dented silver bucket. She observed the other girls watching in disbelief from inside, holding the shutters open to get a good view. Miss Peters ran out from her tiny house to greet the visitors, the girls all close behind. She put her hand up, signaling them to stay back and quiet as the royals climbed from their carriage. Usually Miss Peters' charges knew it was better to follow her direction than to suffer her punishment. But the draw of a glimpse of the young prince, on their turf no less, made them inch ever closer. Ginny knew her place and hung back. The orphanage only received a handful of random visitors a year. Occasionally a new girl arrived to stay, necessitating the food to stretch further for another mouth. The arrival of the king was surprising and out of place. Royalty belonged at the castle, not in front of a ramshackle bedhouse and a farm that smelled of animal feces and a well that gave off more sulfur than water.

"Your Highness," Miss Peters said, curtseying in front of the group.

"My dear lady, might I trouble you for a few moments of your time?" the king addressed her directly.

"Of course, Your Majesty," she replied, only bowing her head this time. One of the knights gave a sharp command. At this, they all dismounted their horses. A lone knight removed his helmet and directed the king and prince in front of Miss Peters. She led them into her humble dwelling as the remaining guardsmen busied themselves tying up the horses to trees on the edge of the woods across the tiny lane.

Ginny was closest, so she ran over by the back window in the kitchen that she knew would be open to vent the heat generated from the hearth. She was the first to reach it, but the other girls were close behind. Two tried to push her out of the way, from the right and the left simultaneously, making no progress toward their desired goal. Lydia tried to grab Ginny around her waist and forcibly throw her out of the way, whispering, "Move you fat troll." But Ginny, anticipating this, already had the fingernails of her chubby hands dug into the rotten windowsill. The splinters of wood and peeling paint bit into the tender skin in her nail bed as she felt the sill struggling to hold despite the force. The others packed up against the house behind her.

"My name is Miss Peters, Your Highness," her shaky voice floated out the window. No one dared peek in as they would be dismissed if they were spotted.

The king had asked her name? How did he not have a record of who lived in his kingdom, Ginny wondered.

"Mrs. Peters," the king began.

"No, it is Miss. I never married," she clarified.

Ginny snickered. Miss Peters had no patience for poor listeners.

"Right, my apologies. It is common knowledge in the villages, but as you live way out here in isolation, you may not have heard. As you appear to be an educated woman, I am sure you are aware of the finer details of the curse."

"Yes, Your Highness."

"As my dear boy is coming of age, we have been having line-ups at the castle, where all the women come to kiss the prince. I realize not every resident makes it to those occasions. I've decided to take my boy around the countryside to search for this mythical most beautiful female that the witch prophesized. I know no better way to find our solution than by process of elimination..."

"Oh, listen to how fancy he talks," Melissa sighed.

Ginny only snorted. He was admitting he could do no more than guess at a solution to a huge issue that affected the welfare of thousands of people. Melissa, and most likely the king himself, didn't realize this was not an intelligent statement, and was cause for major concern for all their destinies.

The king continued inside, "When we pulled up, I noticed you house a fair amount of girls. The prince needs to kiss each one of them to try to break the curse."

At that moment, all the adolescents behind Ginny screamed loudly in anticipation of kissing the prince, giving them away. Miss Peters got up, ran over to the window and shooed them all away. They scattered like the chickens when it was time to start cooking Sunday dinner. But Ginny remained directly below the window, under the sill. Miss Peters had not seen her.

It didn't seem fair. Ginny had thought at first the king had come to ferret out the thieves. Instead the thieves would get to make out with his son.

"Of course, Your Highness."

Like she really had any choice in the matter.

"Please, line them up. We will be out in a moment after I prepare the prince."

"Yes, Your Highness." The sound of the door opening and closing on the front of the cottage could be heard. All that remained in the room were the king, the prince, and the knight.

"Dad, I don't want to do this."

"Jeremie, it is your royal duty."

"It is my royal duty to kiss a bunch of strange women? Doesn't that sound wrong to you?"

"It is life with the curse. It is a necessary evil."

"I don't understand why that mean old witch cursed our kingdom in the first place," the prince whined helplessly.

"We may never know, son," the king confided.

The front door opened and they all exited. She crept around the side of the house to watch. Ginny stifled a giggle. Lydia and the others looked like cows lined up for the slaughter.

Miss Peters presented each girl in turn to the prince. He kissed every one, looking a bit more defeated with each lip lock. Every girl smiled a goofy smile, and then pranced off to join the others who were already finished. They were busy comparing who had the best kiss with the handsome prince. The momentous thrill distracted them from the obvious. It would not dawn on them until they were tucked into their straw mattress beds tonight that none of them had broken the curse. None of these dirt poor orphans would wake up in the castle tomorrow as a princess.

After the kiss-a-thon, Miss Peters sent all the girls back to the dorm. Then she prepared lunch for the king. In these hard times, the kitchen only had a miniscule stock of desirable foods, such as beef, cheese, and sugar. Miss Peters would surely feed them all to the king to please him and earn his favor. The others paid no attention to stock levels in the kitchen pantry or where their food came from. But Ginny did. She suspected this royal visit would cost them dearly.

While the king and his right-hand man dined inside, the rest of the royal guard lounged across the road on nature's carpet of soft grass, eating jerkified meat from their packs. Miss Peters had herded the other orphans into the bedhouse to keep them out of site and trouble. She had not seen Ginny by the side of the house. Not that it mattered anyway. She would know that Ginny would not cause any problems. Ginny fetched some water from the well, offering it up to the relaxing guards. The first guard took some, but unhappily drank it when he realized it was tainted. The other guards thanked her, but declined.

All the hub-bub temporarily at a standstill, Ginny returned to the barn to finish tending to the cows, chickens, and pigs. Climbing over a bale of hay, she exclaimed in surprise as she found someone lounging.

"Sorry to scare you. I figured I had some time to kill while my dad chowed down," the prince responded.

"Oh, it's fine. Uh, Your Highness. I just didn't... Sorry." It occurred to Ginny that it must be strange to be able to address the king of the land as simply "dad." Really, addressing anyone as dad seemed simply bizarre to Ginny with her upbringing.

"I can leave if you want me to," he said with a smile, knowing she did not.

"No, you are free to stay as long as you like, of course. It is your kingdom, after all."

"My family may rule the kingdom, but I want you to know I still believe in everyone's personal property. My dad could be in there a while. He really likes to eat."

"I was afraid of that. Oh, I didn't mean that," she said, throwing her chubby hand over her mouth.

Instead of being mad, Jeremie bent over laughing. He wiped tears from his eyes and composed himself.

"I'm very sorry," she attempted an apology.

"No, don't be. I never get to talk to anyone who tells it like it is. It is refreshing."

"I've been called a lot of names before, but 'refreshing' is not one of them."

He chuckled again although what she said had not really been all that amusing. No one ever laughed at what she said the way he was. He didn't find amusement in her embarrassment, as the others always did. He seemed to truly enjoy her company. But then again, the only person Ginny ever engaged in average daily conversation with was Miss Peters, and she found nothing amusing. Ever.

When she didn't go on, Jeremie continued. "You come with your caregiver and the other girls to the market regularly, don't you? I recognize you," he said easily.

"I'm hard to miss," Ginny shrunk a few steps back from the care-free distance she had been from the prince. She remembered then who and what she was, how she must look to him. She cringed, remembering the beast that had stared back at her from the reflection of the cracked mirror this morning.

"What is your name?"

"Guinevere. But everyone just calls me Ginny."

"Whatever for?" he paused. "How old are you?"

It was a nice, normal question that put her breathing at ease.

"Thirteen. I'll be fourteen next month."

"I just turned thirteen. Seems we have something in common then." He smiled at her.

"The only thing," she muttered, half under her breath.

"Prince Jeremie!" The startled cry rang out across the small pasture and into the barn. Here they were, Jeremie relaxing on a hay bale with a book and Ginny standing awkwardly in front of him.

"I think your disappearance has been noticed," she informed him.

"It was bound to happen eventually. It took them longer this time than most," he explained to her, then stood up. He made it sound as though he escaped their watch as often as possible. This made her curious. She would have liked to hear more about that. Cupping a hand around his mouth, he called, "I'm in here." Then to Ginny, he said, "I'll expect to see you at the market sometime soon?" He flashed his bright white-toothed smile at her.

It was hard, but Ginny forced her mouth to stay shut and not to return the smile, hiding her own crooked teeth. She acknowledged him with a nod. Then the same guard who gone with the king into the house rushed into the small barn, momentarily blocking the single ray of sunlight flowing in the door. She recognized him by his brown moustache. But the eclipse wasn't enough for Ginny to miss the cringe he had at his first glimpse of her appearance. She somehow managed to shrink up even further.

"Master, how dare you worry us all like that!" he exclaimed. His breathes were deep with the exertion of running as he quickly went to work brushing hay off the purple velvet overcoat of the prince.

"Oh ya, Merrick, I'm sure my father was sooo worried," he replied sarcastically, winking at Ginny.

"His majesty is already waiting in the carriage."

The king was so heavy, Ginny wondered how the carriage was able to bear his weight.

The man she now knew was named Merrick wrapped his arm around Jeremie, quickly ushering him from her vicinity. She could have walked to the door and watched him leave, but she did not. She wanted to remember their sweet encounter, just as it had been.

At the dinner table, over a meal of nothing but boiled turnips and potatoes, the others mocked her.

"Really Ginny! While you were out wallowing with the pigs, we all got to kiss the prince!" Natalie informed her. Her cheeks were positively crimson with the added blush of excitement.

"Yes, anyone who might be the most beautiful woman in the land," Angie snickered.

"And we all know that that could *never* be you!" Lydia chuckled.

Ginny kept her mouth shut, taking measured bites and chewing them completely until they were no more than cud. She was trying to trick her stomach into believing she was putting more food into it than she actually was.

She heard every taunting word they said, but she pretended not to. She should be used to this treatment, her skin metaphorically scarred from the daily abuse of their verbal diarrhea, the words cutting like knives. Usually the words never stopped piercing, not even when she was asleep, as they even haunted her nightmares. Tonight, though, they could not reach one place: a small, warm spot in her belly. Ginny imagined it looking like one metallic fleck, maybe sparkling, containing her brief conversation with Jeremie. She would not tell the other girls. They would never believe her. And she didn't want to give them the power to take that small happiness away from her, as they surely could with just a few clicks of their sharp tongues.

**H**ey, Troll. Trisha left the bathtub for ya. Just head on out," Lydia said, a small smile crossing her lips as she turned her head. Ginny didn't think too much about it. Lydia was always incredibly amused with herself. She was highly intelligent, but only used it for cruel intentions.

It was Sunday morning, when they usually had their weekly baths. Sometimes Ginny snuck through the woods down to the creek to take hers. It gave her an iota of privacy. Plus, she didn't have to worry about any of the other girls making fun of her. But it was the middle of winter, and the creek was frozen over, so that wasn't an option at present.

During the cold months the tub was set up in the barn, where at least the wind and snow didn't hit her while she was wet, making her ever colder. The water was boiled in the fireplace initially, but only the first couple bathers benefited from that, either the oldest or the most aggressive. Ginny had always been at the bottom of the hierarchy in the bedhouse, and she wasn't about to put a larger target on her back by starting a dispute about something as silly as cleaner and warmer bath water. Ginny frowned at the thought that Trisha had been in most recently. She was not much more than a baby and often peed in it.

Ginny made her way to the barn, on the snow-packed path that the other girls had already flattened with her shoes, as equally holey as Ginny's were. She opened the door, and then quickly closed it behind herself, which blocked out all the natural sunlight. There was only one lantern lit in the barn and oddly it was not the one closest to the tub. Ginny could take the time to light the one closest, but instead she began to undress. She really wanted to get this over with so she wouldn't have to deal with it again for a week. Maybe it would be spring by then: fat chance.

It smelled worse than usual in here, but that was due to the door being shut and the animals defecating in here more than they did in the summer months. It didn't bother Ginny much, as she would be the one out here tomorrow to remove it. She heard the intermittent sounds of the animals chewing, snoring, and grunting. Their hooves scraped against the dirt floor, restless.

The tub was filled quite full today, but that wasn't unusual this time of year. The latter girls would try to dump in more boiling water to reheat it, but it never worked. Once the metal cooled down, you were sunk.

Ginny tried to glance inside before stepping in, but the tub was dark to begin with, and the lack of light made it look like a black, liquid surface. She shrugged and climbed in, one foot first, then the other. The first foot sunk deeply into something that was thicker than water. She tried to reverse direction quickly, but her inertia and whatever was in the tub sucked her down, actually causing her to lose balance and slip right into it. She fell into the gooey substance against her will, a shriek coming out of her mouth.

This was quickly followed by the hysterical laughter of all the other orphans. They ran out from behind the stalls and piles of hay and feeding troughs that they had been concealing themselves behind. They pointed and screamed as Ginny climbed out as quickly as she could. The texture and the scent left no doubt that they had filled the tub with pig manure. She was already crying, and really just wanted to get the feces off of her as quickly as possible.

But one should always be careful what one wishes for. No sooner had Ginny had that thought than Lydia and two other girls threw buckets of water at her. They must have been keeping them outside, because they were so cold that her skin felt raw as the water slammed into it. She screamed again, then realized she was standing there entirely nakid, cold, shivering in front of all these bullies who hated her for nothing more than being herself.

Her body quickly heated up with the shame she felt, standing there exposed like that. Her skin was on fire. Maybe a normal person would have been mad at their tormentors. But Ginny was only mad at herself. Red hot rage directed inward, clouding her sight. Embarrassment oozed out of her every pore. She felt dirty, but no shower could rid her of this shame. It would be added on to all the other incidents piled up inside her brain, the years and years of mental scars. Even when she couldn't separate each instance into its own individual memories, the emotions and the toll it took on her self-esteem was still there. She felt like slime. It didn't seem possible that she could continue to live on this planet feeling this worthless. But her lungs continued to push air and her heart continued to pump blood. No natural force was striking her down where she stood. No chain of events had killed her with a runaway wagon. So she existed, miserably.

Ginny scooped up her clothes, and swung open the barn door, running for the house as quickly as she could, their cackles seeming to only grow louder behind her. She was too upset to be uncomfortable with the cold beneath her nakid feet, but was cognizant of the fact that it was cleaning the rest of the pig crap from her feet and ankles. This only reminded her that she had inadvertently abandoned her shoes in the barn. The others would no doubt steal or burn then. She anticipated wrapping her feet in rags tomorrow to venture out into the winter to complete her farmyard chores.

She ran into the bedhouse, flinging the door shut behind her. She ran over to the corner of the room, slamming her back into the wall as she slid down it to rest on the floor. Tears, now cold and grainy, began to air dry on her cheeks that burned like a frying pan on the fire. She sat, feeling as if there was no reason to still be here and no purpose in life. She didn't even bother to put her clothes back on yet. She was thankful that her tormentors did not follow her. She skipped lunch and dinner to avoid them, but they were all early to bed and talked half the night about what a great prank it had been, right in front of her as if she was not even there.

To make matters worse, Miss Peters went to the barn before Ginny made it out there in the morning. She was furious about the mess in the bathing tub. All the girls blamed Ginny and she didn't bother to argue. It would be useless anyway. Either way she would be the one to clean it. But unfortunately, being in Miss Peters bad graces, she received less food and more chores. And the real culprits escaped punishment entirely.

The next occasion they went to market, Ginny was actually excited to go. There were early fruits and flowers and herbs to take for sale or trade, along with the candles the orphans had spent long, cold winter days making cooped up indoors, trying to fight boredom but losing. The newly-sprouted woods they traveled through gave hope for an improved year ahead in all matters. Sure, there were still the children, and adults, who pointed and snickered at her appearance. But the chance to see the prince again made the exposure more bearable. He had not made an appearance at the previous market day they had attended at harvest. Ginny had not seen him since the chat they had shared in the barn.

The king and the prince walked through as the market opened. It was early and Ginny was still helping Miss Peters set up and the other girls had not had time to run off to the other booths yet.

In fact, Ginny was right out in front of their booth setting up baskets, a spot she would not usually put herself in. But she had been so eagerly waiting to see the prince, to see if he would acknowledge her, that she had forgotten all she had learned through past experience about not making herself a target for humiliation.

The pair of royals passed their booth before Jeremie looked back, spotting her. He stopped in his tracks, turning toward her, his father made to look the fool as he continued on without his son for several steps.

"Hey, Guinevere. I hope you and your caretaker were granted safe travels today."

"Yes, thank you. Your Majesty, of course," Ginny fumbled. The king, more overweight than Ginny remembered and looking larger yet in close proximity, tugged at the prince's elbow, ushering him along. She noticed that he did not ask about any of the other girls.

"Have a prosperous day at market."

"Thank you," she replied reflexively. She gave him a slight wave, but he had already turned back to his father.

Lydia grabbed Ginny's hand mid-wave and bent it backwards, the sickening snap of bone vibrating up her arm. Ginny tried to scream out, but Natalie came up from behind and shoved an apple in her mouth, silencing her like a roasted pig.

"What was that all about *Gwin-ever-ear*," Lydia snarled, drawing out and mispronouncing her given name so that it sounded as ugly as Ginny looked.

"Don't you know it is *nas-tee* for ugly old trolls to talk to princes?" Natalie said, trying to imitate Lydia, but failing miserably. That kind of evil incarnate can't be learned.

"Ya. He is looking for the most beautiful girl in the land. You are like, so totally the opposite of that," Lydia growled.

They held her so tightly she could not wiggle free. They even stood on top of her feet, having learned from past fights that Ginny was an excellent kicker, especially to their shins.

"They are right," Miss Peters's voice sounded from behind them. "You should not be bothering the royal family. It is inexcusable."

Miss Peters never stood up for her. Ginny was a rabbit caught by a pack of wolves.

"See? We are right. You are too ugly to even be in his gorgeous presence," Natalie cooed.

"Maybe you need a permanent reminder about your place, troll," Lydia sneered.

Fast as lightning Lydia drug her pocket knife across Ginny's face. The burning went from the left ear, deep into her cheek, and across the end of her nose. An irritating warm stickiness left a pulling sensation in its wake as it moved down toward her jawline. Lydia and Natalie let go of her then and ran, their shoes with holes in the soles slapping the cobblestones.

Ginny stood there, her uninjured hand holding her injured face. Miss Peters walked up behind her, putting her hand on Ginny's right shoulder, where the blood wouldn't drip on it.

"Maybe now you will remember this important lesson," she stated knowingly, like a school teacher instructing students on the Pythagorean Theorem.

Oh yes, Ginny would remember this lesson she learned today.

She learned to never to open herself up to that kind of torment again. Ginny's secrets and joys would have to remain just that—all her own.

# SHE GRINS

She grins,
a crooked, yellow & white spotted grin
I stare back
how can she not realize how ugly
she be
Eyebrows like Gorillas
A nose the size of a Redwood
Has a boyfriend?
He MUST be blind
Greasy, unattractive hair
not shampoo commercial model quality
Pulls it back
ponytail so tight
beaky nose juts out more
Why did her parents let her be born
Glasses too
cursed by the gods
of Hell, that is
Make her stop staring at me
Stop me from seeing her face
It doesn't fit together
Left Over Used Parts
Go away, bitch.

And I walked away from the mirror.

When fall came, and there were vegetables and flour ground from grains to take to market, Ginny remained at the orphanage. Miss Peters told her it would be for the best. Ginny couldn't help but think it was because of her scar, still fresh and ugly after four months of infections preventing a proper healing. Miss Peters had bound her wrist until it could mend properly, but there was not much to be done for Ginny's face. When she had thought she couldn't get any uglier, Lydia had showed her that anything was possible. If only seeing the prince again was.

She could not help herself. She watched as the old rickety wagon with the borrowed horse filled with heinous girls and only a handful of wares bumped off down the road, leaving her behind. They all waved and laughed at her.

Alone.

That is how she had started her life in a basket. Why should anything in her existence ever change? The tears flowed freely. There was no reason to try and conceal them. She went up to the hayloft in the barn to hide, which was silly, because there was no one to hide from. The others would not return until dark. She fell into a fitful sleep, but was awakened when she heard a persistent knocking coming from outside.

When she peeked out the barn door, she could see a wagon parked in front of Miss Peters's cottage. It had writing on it, but she couldn't read it from her present position. Whoever was knocking must belong with the wagon. She couldn't see the front of the house from here either. It would be easy enough to just hide and wait for the stranger to leave. But it was unusual for anyone to travel out away from the villages this far, and that peaked Ginny's curiosity.

She knew it was dangerous to talk to strangers when she was a young girl all alone. Anything could happen. It was even more so with her unusual looks. If she startled the wrong person, she knew they could kill her instantly. But maybe that appeal was exactly what possessed Ginny to leave her hiding place and approach the house. When she rounded the corner, she could see the back of a man in a well-worn suit and top hat. He had given up knocking for now and was stroking his pair of horses, as if in preparation to remount and leave.

"What can I help you with, sir?" Ginny's voice was small, but the man still jumped at the unexpected sound. Turning, she saw him startle again as if someone had hit him when he laid eyes on her appearance.

"Oh! I didn't think anyone was at home. Are you the lady of the house?"

It sounded strange that anyone should think she could ever be the lady of any house. No one would marry her or take her on as a servant. Ginny was doomed to live out the rest of her days here at the orphanage. She had made her peace with that fate long ago. But today this man was giving her a chance to be whoever she wanted to be. Maybe it was time to play a different role.

"I am today," she finally answered him.

A smile lit up his face, making his cheeks rosy. His white moustache, curled at the ends, accentuated them. He took off his top hat to bow, revealing more white hair that had been concealed underneath it.

"Glad to hear it! I would love to take a few moments of your time and show you some of the exquisite products I carry with me today. I am sorry, but I did not catch your name little Miss."

"Ginny. My name is Ginny." She could plainly tell now that his wagon read: Fred Dejarlais – Fabulous Finds, Festive Wares, Medicinal Remedies.

"Miss Ginny, I bring to you today some of the most exquisite and exotic treasures from as far as the emperors in Egypt and the darkest jungles of the Amazon. Any problem that you may encounter in your daily life, be it an itchy insect bite, a broken wagon wheel, a dog due to whelp, or a fireplace kettle that doesn't shine quite like it used to, I have the solution right in here." He slapped his hand against the painted boards of his wagon. He gave a charismatic delivery and he had Ginny's attention. She had ninety-nine problems and would love to be able to solve any one of them. His eyes twinkled above his rosy, round cheeks as he spoke. Gauging her interest, he now swung open the doors on the side of his wagon.

Ginny gasped. She had never seen so many beautiful items all stacked together before in her life. The first thing her eyes locked onto was a toy bear. The salesman, implementing years of experience, picked up on that right away. He grabbed it down at once and handed it to her.

"Real rabbit fur over ground nutshells. The button eyes are made of genuine onyx."

She almost dropped it at the unexpected texture. It was soft in her hands, like holding a cloud. As she rubbed her hands down its white, jointed arm, Ginny instantly felt calmer. He was a friend who would never leave her, never laugh at her. Security.

"There a little one in your life that might like that, Miss?"

Just like that, Ginny was snapped out of her fantasy and quickly handed it back to him. He had pointed out the obvious. At fifteen, she was too old for childish things. She would never be able to keep it safe and out of the other girls' hands. Ginny's heart broke for something she was never meant to have. He took down pots and pans to show her, some painted in bright, cheery colors. But the things that sparkled in the mid-day sun really got her attention. The perceptive man pulled down a scarf she had been studying. It was thin, for dressing up, not for winter warmth, and totally impractical for farm work. But the fabric had every color she had ever seen, finished with gold and silver threads running through it. Ginny did not even know how you made gold or silver into thread.

"Ah, a quality item. Shall I wrap it up for ya?" he asked, salivating. It was what Miss Peters would refer to on other women as "tacky," but Ginny loved it. She would have to hide it and never be able to wear it. Would it be worth it?

"Yes," she responded, ignoring her common sense screaming that it was stupid.

"Now, you know, with a scarf that fancy, most women would wear cosmetics."

"Cosmetics?" Ginny asked naïvely.

"You know—makeup, face paint, lipstick, rouge."

"Oh yes," she replied, smiling in realization. The other girls talked about such things, but they didn't own any. Miss Peters would never allow it.

"The kit I have today is jam-packed with everything you need to get started on your journey to beauty. We have base, blush, eye paste, liner for eyes and lips, lipstick, and, of course, remover. It can make a monkey look like a zebra, a girl look like a woman, a homely maid into a future princess."

Princess. Prince Jeremie. Maybe makeup was Ginny's answer to look respectable enough to go to market again, to see the prince.

"Does it hide scars?" she asked breathlessly, absent-mindedly holding the scarf over her own.

"Oh, my lady. It will hide wrinkles, pimples, pustules, blisters, bumps, birthmarks, horse fly bites, wayward brands, pock marks, blotches, scrapes, and even scars."

"I'll take it!" Ginny cried.

"I will just need funds from you to complete the transaction."

"Of course. I'll go get it."

The salesman was befuddled as Ginny, instead of heading into the cottage they were standing in front of, ran off to the long house next door.

What if this was the solution she had needed all along? What if it could not only hide her scar, but make her look *normal*, like other women? She could fit in, not have strangers startle at her appearance. What if she could be, heaven-forbid, beautiful?

Ginny could not get the few coins she had stowed away in the secret hiding spot of the sole of her winter boots fast enough. She sprinted back out to the man and presented him with payment. His demeanor instantly darkened as he counted the coins.

"Hey, you said you wanted the scarf *and* the makeup. There isn't enough money here for both."

"But I don't have any more money," she explained, feeling like the dirty, insignificant orphan that she was.

"Look kid, don't waste my time here. I thought we had a good relationship going."

Yes, Ginny had thought the same thing.

"In times such as these, I will also offer trades, out of the kindness of my heart. Do you have some jewelry you could part with, perhaps?"

"No sir. I have nothing of the sort."

"How about your grandmother, or an aunt? They got something you could provide me with?"

Ginny wanted that makeup more than life itself, but not enough to steal from Miss Peters.

"No, sir."

"Well, then I guess I will have to put these items back on the rack and be on my way," he said, turning his back to her.

"No! Uh, how about I only buy the makeup?"

"Well, if you're sure. But it would really look better with the scarf too, if you could swing it."

"No, no. Just the makeup will be fine." Ginny quickly snatched the small case from him and ran toward the dormitory with it, leaving him holding the scarf in one hand and her payment in the other.

She unlatched the case on her mattress and looked inside, the sound of horses' hooves fading into the distance beyond her open window.

Luckily all the bottles and jars were labeled, so she would know what went where on her face. She took the bottle marked "base" over to the cracked mirror affixed to the wall. She poured a puddle of the tan goo into her hand, and then smeared it about her face. After much blending, it did hide her scar and a few other blemishes. But her nose still bulged and her eyelids still drooped. Maybe the eye parts would help that. She took out the eye liner, and began to draw around her eyes with it. It smelled like charcoal from the fire and made great smudges around her optical orbs. Her chubby hands were shaking, causing her lines to look like they had been applied by a child. Ginny sat back and surveyed her cracked reflection. She looked like a raccoon that had crawled down the chimney.

She applied, in turn, the blush, then the lipstick. Ginny could tell it was still her trollish face that stared back at her, albeit more colorful. She decided maybe she hadn't used *enough* blush and lipstick. When she was still not satisfied with her new and improved appearance, she got out the eye paste. It was thick. It was hard for her to rub it on her sagging eyelids with her fingers. She found a brush in the kit that worked only marginally better. The paste was cerulean and sparkly. It reminded her of fish scales when they were sliced off the filet for dinner. She thought on her eyelids it looked more purple, like a fresh bruise administered by Lydia's fist. But it was hard to tell, as where it had entered her eyes it was now burning. Tears spilled out, and down her freshly painted cheeks.

Is this any girl that the prince would want? There was only a monster staring back at her. She continued crying, running to her bed. She threw herself onto it, knocking the tiny bottles off onto the floor, a few breaking, a few spilling.

This is how Miss Peters found her when they returned from market. Miss Peters reprimanded her for her foolish behavior in a stern tone.

"Ginny, how could you purchase items from a peddler? *How many times* have I warned you against it? But you did not listen. They will tell you whatever you want to hear. It is all a falsehood. They have nothing that you need. They cannot be trusted."

"Did you do that yourself?" Angie snorted cruelly.

"It's not going to help! There is nothing to help that ugly old troll face!" Lydia bellowed.

They laughed so long and hard that most of them made almost no noise at all, struggling for breath. Minnie, a new arrival who came malnourished and had yet to put on weight, fainted.

Ginny was thankful for one thing: she could not see their reactions. Her eyes had been swollen shut for hours. Water would not wash this junk off, and the bottle of remover that came in the kit had only been a bottle of equine urine. Now Ginny was not only just as ugly, but also blind and smelled of horse piss. Somedays it didn't pay to get out of bed.

The makeup had caused an allergic reaction with her skin. It was red and irritated and starting to weep terribly, which made the itching even fiercer. They could not even begin to calm the allergy until they could get the makeup removed. Miss Peters had to use the strongest solvent in the house to get it off. This only led to more skin irritation. Poor Ginny was miserable. Thankfully, once the swelling went down around her eyes she was able to see again. She was confined to bed for three whole days. She still didn't feel well on the fourth, but she was the workhorse of the lot and the other girls refused to pick up the slack.

When all was said and done, Ginny's complexion actually looked markedly worse after the cosmetics debacle than it had before. She could not win for trying. She was the biggest lost cause ever.

A few weeks later, Ginny dreamed that a frog kissed her and she turned into a beautiful girl. She knew how silly it was the moment she awakened. Ladies were supposed to kiss frogs to make them princes, not the other way around. But she couldn't stop her heart from aching when she blinked back the first rays of the morning sun. She wanted beauty, badly. It would be the key to friends, a husband, and a normal life. It should have been a happy dream, but the loss of it felt like a sledgehammer to her gut. Miss Peters punished her for not getting out of bed on time, and again later for not completing her chores. Although it was now clearly day, she could not shake the melancholy that the loss of the dream had left her with. She was so out of sorts she made the mistake of letting her guard down and telling Natalie she had had a bad dream. Sometime that evening between dinner and bed, some unknown girl, most likely Lydia or all of them together, stole her straw mattress off her bed and burned it. That night she lay on the cold floor, sleep, and a replay of the dream, eluding her.

Sometimes she thought that being beautiful would not only heal her heart, but the whole kingdom as well. Stupid dreams for a stupid troll gurl to dream, she guessed.

Ginny's life went on day-to-day, a monotonous blur of chores and torment at the hands of her so-called sisters. She learned to love reading as an escape, but she could seldom finish one book before another girl took it away, usually destroying it. They found reading to be foolish, and most of them never even bothered to learn. The books came from Miss Peters's bookshelf. When they stopped being returned, she forbade Ginny from borrowing any more.

Ginny did not go to the next market day. She didn't really care if she ever went again. They lived so far away from the castle, it was easy to forget that they were even ruled by a buffoonish king and a handsome prince.

Almost.

Until one day a posse road up to their door. It was smaller this time. No royal flagmen were present, but there were several guards. There was no king's carriage, only men on horses, two being younger than the rest. Ginny was outside with the animals, so she was first to approach.

There were disparaging human titters along with the usual horse ones as she approached.

"Hey, Guinevere," the prince's voice rang out above everyone else, the tone as easy as if he were playing sports with his chums.

Ginny never thought she would see him again, especially here where she lived. He dismounted his horse. Remembering her manners, she bowed before him and replied, "Your Majesty."

"Please, call me Jeremie. We were heading to the Outlands. Thought we might stop here and water the horses for a moment."

Ginny looked over the motley crew out on their travels. The adult men didn't stop staring at Ginny or whispering to one another. It was as if she was a farm animal with two asses, like they thought she wouldn't hear their words or be hurt by them. But she had learned a long time ago that that was what everyone assumed; that she was deaf and dumb and nothing more than an animal, not a human as they were. Maybe she really was some type of mythical troll. But then shouldn't she be special and revered?

The only two not joining in the gossip were the prince and the other young man. He had on a hat that he removed as he held his horse in place. It revealed short-cropped blond hair. He had light blue eyes that were his most prominent feature, haunted with a deep sadness. He had a thin nose and full, pink lips that he used to give commands to his steed. He was handsome in his own right. Ginny imagined if he had been traveling alone, he would have attracted the attention of every girl at the orphanage. But while traveling in the presence of the prince, his fine traits were overshadowed.

"Of course, Your Majesty." Her glance met his warm brown eyes and tried to keep a silly grin off her face and her knees from shaking.

"Hey, we are still doing that line up business to break the curse. Are there any new girls since I was here last?"

"Oh, I believe one or two. I could get Miss Peters for you," Ginny turned her head toward the dormitory to fetch her, but her and the others were already heading their way to greet the royal caravan. Ginny backed away then, knowing her place in society was behind them all. Whereas the prince had approached Ginny, all the rude harpies swarmed the poor prince. So much so that two of the guards had to forcefully push them back. It was really kind of greedy, them all competing for his attention and favor. After a few minutes of discussions, Miss Peters lined the pretty lasses up. Jeremie kissed them all, even though some he had before, just to be sure no one was missed.

The guardsmen prepared the horses to depart. Miss Peters insistently herded the girls back to the dorms, but a few hung back to try to wink at the prince or touch the medals on his traveling coat. While Miss Peters busied herself with them, she never noticed that Ginny was lagging behind. Always the quiet one, she had opportunities to observe things the others never would—a mouse hoarding away for winter hibernation, a vulture making dinner of the vibrant red innards of a dead otter, a one on one with the prince.

"I haven't seen you in the market lately. Have you been ill?"

"No, no." Damned her honest tongue. It would have been the easiest answer, to lie. "I had a lot of work to do around the farm is all."

"Ahh," he nodded as if in understanding, although she knew damn well he had never done farm work a day in his life.

"I wanted to go, but, ya, well," she stuttered.

"Hey, what happened to your cheek? It looks like you got a little scratch there. You OK?"

Ginny was in turn embarrassed and flattered. Of course she was mortified he had indeed noticed that her hideousness had only gotten worse. But it did not go unnoticed to her that this was the second time he had been concerned about her health in as many minutes.

"Oh that," her hand flew up to her cheek. "It was, well..." She didn't want to lie, although once again it would be the easier choice. She didn't want the prince to realize how pathetic she really was. But he would figure it out on his own soon enough. She might as well come clean. "Some of the girls, there was a disagreement, and well, it didn't work out well for me," she concluded, leaving out any details related to him.

"Really? Those girls? Why?" he said, miffed. He really had no idea how people could be.

"It sounds like your parents haven't explained the circle of life to you."

"The birds and the bees, I know all about that," he chuckled. Ginny blushed and smiled, but continued.

"No, not like that." She took a deep breath and forged ahead. "Out here, beyond the castle walls, it is predator versus prey. Survival of the fittest. The best-looking and strongest animals get mates and have babies, while the deformed or sick ones are food for the vultures. People are much the same way. If they see you as weaker, they will dominate you to their advantage."

"So, you are implying you are near the bottom of this hierarchy in that little brain of yours?"

"Yes."

"Why would you ever think that?"

"It is obvious. All the girls can see it."

"Why do you let them treat you that way?"

"They are better than me. No one ever wanted me. That is how I ended up here; just a dirty little orphan girl."

"No, they are not better. They are orphans, same as you, no matter how they got here." Ginny had never thought of it that way before. He had rendered her silent in their conversation as he mounted his chestnut horse.

"I am glad I was able to see you on this visit. I hope you will be at the market on the first."

"I would have to check with Miss Peters," Ginny stumbled over her words.

"Then we shall leave it as a maybe. I bid you good day."

None of the girls must have witnessed the exchange with the prince, because no knife cut her flesh that evening.

Troll became a nickname that stuck. And Ginny could not entirely argue that it was not suitable. As they matured, the other adolescents sprouted curves, which eventually landed many of them husbands. Or at the least a ride into the next town and away from the orphanage. Their faces thinned, losing their baby fat. They grew great, cute noses and bright oval eyes. They became tall and leggy and beautiful. Any of them might end up to be the one who could take the prince's hand and break the spell.

Ginny grew to look, well, more troll-like. She still sometimes believed that maybe one of her parents had actually been a troll. Miss Peters assured her this was not the case. But if she had been left on the doorstep, then how could Miss Peters be sure of that?

Her giant nose grew larger. Her eyelids sagged lower over her eyes, still more on the right than the left. Her forehead got bigger and wrinklier, while her hair hung stick straight, the color of unpleasant mud. Her left cheek grew bigger than the other, both outsizing her face and covered in acne. She tried never to open her mouth, for her adult teeth had all snagged and snarled against each other. They were yellow, which would have been bad enough, but they also had white spots on them, which only intensified the ugly yellow-ness. She had grown not one, not two, but three growths on her face that were not only ugly, but dark hair sprouted out of them as well.

Where the other girls had grown curves, Ginny only became stocky and thick. She remained an average height for a girl, but developed a hunch in her back which robbed her once again of any normalcy. She had large, wide feet, and stubby fingers. But she was grateful every day that they worked. Ginny was terrified that if one day she woke up and her arms and legs had become gnarled to a point where she could not use them, there would be no one to do the work and they all would starve to death.

Unbeknownst to Ginny as she sat in the booth on their day at the market tying candles together (sold to the elderly who could no longer make them due to arthritis and bad eye sight or the wealthy who chose not to), Lydia was in the back garden of the castle. She had snuck back there to make out with Chester, a much older man in the "entertainment business."

"Are your shows very popular?" she asked. She didn't appreciate his beard scratching up her face.

"Oh, people come from miles around to attend."

"How will you leave Inniskellin? The other lands don't allow travel from here."

"I sneak in and out in the dead of night. I am not the only one. I have a right to conduct my business however I want to," he said, cockily. They resumed their heated kissing.

"Is it music? Art?" Lydia broke her liplock long enough to inquire. She had always dreamed of being a famous show girl. Maybe he would be her ride out of this dying kingdom.

"No, no. Much edgier. Think more like a zoo."

"A zoo? Ew."

"Of people," Chester replied, as if it should have been obvious.

"That is stupid. I can see people any old day of the week."

"No, you don't understand. These are unique specimens I have collected from all over the world," he explained.

"Speci-mins?"

"I have an African tribesman with the longest neck you have ever seen. I have a teenage boy with two heads. I have an oriental with her feet bound so tight she hasn't been able to walk in years. I have a collection of shrunken heads, ginormous teeth, and deformed genitalia. I make a *fortune* off these people," Chester bragged.

"I don't see how you can make much after you pay them."

"Who says I pay them? I provide food and travel. What more could they want? They don't even have feelings. They are *freaks*."

"Oh, I see."

"Ya, people are always attracted to natural oddities. I have a dog with two tails. They both wag. The little kiddies always get a kick out of that," he paused. "I just wish I could find something new and fresh. I would hate to think I already have all there is to be seen."

"Wait, you want a freak? I fuckin' live with one!"

"You do?! How long will it take us to get to it?" He was almost salivating.

"She is across the square right now."

"Take me to her."

Lydia and Chester snuck out from their hideaway behind the castle, rushing until she could point out Ginny from behind a row of impeccably trimmed hedges.

"Oh my God, what did you say you call her?"

"She has a name, but I just call her Troll Gurl."

"Oh," Chester said, grasping his hands in front of his mouth and exhaling excitedly. "That thing is perfect."

"Do I get some sort of finder's fee?"

"Hold on, honey. We have to see how easy it is to capture first."

"Just wave a donut in front of her, she will follow you anywhere."

"It likes those, huh?"

"Uh, well. I dunno. None of us have really ever had one. Do you sell them at your shows?"

"Of course we do."

"I would love to see your show." Now Lydia was salivating. She hadn't had anything at all to eat today.

"Ya, ya. We will make a plan to do that sometime."

"Sometime? What about now?"

"Shut up, sweetie. I can see a goldmine in front of me. Why don't you lure her outside the castle for me?"

"Why?"

"So I can grab her, you nit-wit," Chester sighed curtly.

"That will be hard. She won't want to leave. She is such a goody-goody."

Lydia didn't like how Chester had started talking to her, but he was still her best bet at leaving that rotten orphanage, and possibly this whole damn condemned kingdom. Ginny aggravated every nerve in Lydia's body, just by existing. Plus, there was that weird way the prince always talked to her, like they were buddies or something. *That* had to be stopped. A lantern lit up in Lydia's brain.

"Wait, I have the perfect way to lure her out."

"Go get 'er."

Lydia sashayed over to their booth.

"Well, I didn't expect to see you until after take down," Miss Peters muttered.

"Oh, well, I wanted to check and see how you were doing."

Ginny wanted to point out that Lydia would never help if they needed it, so why bother to even inquire. But she knew better and held her tongue.

"I'm gonna take Ginny off to show her something."

"Well, then who will be here to assist the old woman?"

"I think I would rather stay," Ginny stuttered. But it was no use. Lydia ran around the table and grabbed Ginny by a stubby arm and began to drag her away. She tried to plead with her eyes to Miss Peters, but the film on her lenses probably totally blocked the message.

"We will only be a minute," Lydia lied easily.

"I don't want to go," Ginny begged, sensing the impending doom in the air.

"It has to do with the prince," she sang in Ginny's ear. They were too far from Miss Peters now for her to hear.

"The prince?"

"He wants to see you."

A Lydia that was trying to "help?" That was most out of character for her. Maybe this was the plague. Maybe it would kill them all by swapping their personalities to be the opposite.

"That, that isn't true. I'm not even supposed to talk to him." Ginny tried to ignore the fact that her heart had sped up at the sound of Jeremie's title, but she could not hide her sweaty armpits or the blush across her cheeks.

"Not true. I've seen you. You chat him up every chance you get. Of course, it is usually out by the barn. Even then, I bet he can smell your stench over that of the animals."

Lydia was finally sounding more like herself. Maybe this wasn't the end of times after all.

"Why are we heading beyond the castle walls?" Ginny asked as they descended a long staircase.

"How are you supposed to have a clandestine meeting under the watchful eyes of the king? Duh."

"Oh" was Ginny's only reply. Lydia pulled her hard enough now that she was afraid she would tumble down the stairs and break her neck. If she landed on Lydia, it might be worth it.

"What's the rush?"

"We must hurry before he changes his mind," Lydia replied.

Ginny no longer felt she was talking about the prince. She tried to pull away as they reached the bottom of the stairs, but Lydia had her hand wrapped around Ginny's arm too tightly. An apathetic guard stood by the entrance, but as long as people were leaving the castle, he appeared to not give a damn. Plus, security would be more lax as it was market day. So, he paid no mind to the hostage situation.

They came around a stone wall and Lydia pulled her to a sudden stop in front of a man Ginny did not know. But, she knew few people in the kingdom as the orphans were sequestered off in the boondocks at the orphanage. Ginny wondered how Lydia knew the man. He looked like a lumberjack that Ginny had seen in a book once, with thick, brown eyebrows and a beard. Except instead of work clothes, this man sported a flashy overcoat that was coming unstitched at the seams from too much wear. She said nothing as the man appraised her up and down, from her stringy, greasy hair down to her stubby, thick legs that ended in huge feet. She still tried to pull away, but Lydia held her firmly in her grasp.

"Well, Chester. What do you think?" Lydia asked excitedly.

"Oh, you were right, Lydia. She is perfect."

"Perfect for what?" Ginny asked, not wanting to know the answer.

"Oh, it talks. What a shame. The customers like it better when they don't. And so do *I*. But that is a problem that I can remedy. And with a voice like that, sheesh, I may be doing the world a favor."

Ginny had spent years agonizing over what she looked like, she had never stopped to wonder about what she sounded like.

Ginny still didn't have a clear picture of exactly what business Chester was in, but she could already surmise he made people slaves and cut out their tongues so they could not complain about it. As gloomy as her day-to-day life was at the orphanage, Ginny really wasn't interested in downgrading to something even less desirable.

She screamed as loud as she could, at the same time stomping hard on Lydia's foot. Instead of letting go, Lydia clamped her other hand over Ginny's mouth to muffle her. With Lydia in a bear hug around her, there wasn't much Ginny could do to escape. She threw herself on the ground, which proved to be an even more vulnerable position. Now the evil man got involved, grabbing her up in his clutches and slapping wrist irons onto her.

"Behave you stupid troll. We have a long walk back to my caravan and the more hassle you give me now, the bigger beating I will give you when we get there."

Ginny whimpered in defeat. She saw no escape. Miss Peters had always made sure she was cared for, but she wouldn't roam the countryside to recover her. And there was, well, no one else. No one else would even realize she had gone. Lydia uncovered her mouth. Tears rolled down her puffy, acne-covered cheeks. She snuffled, but stopped trying to scream.

"What is this about someone beating one of my royal subjects?"

"Jeremie," Ginny breathed, too loudly.

"I told you to shut up," Chester said, slapping her across the face so hard she fell to the cobblestones.

"And now I witness it. And to a dear friend of the crown, no less," he said, his voice oozing authority.

"You are mistaken, My Prince. This is one of the beasts from my traveling sideshow. It escaped. I was trying to recover it before it caused a scene in the market. Wouldn't want anyone getting harmed, of course…"

"You speak of preventing harm, yet you have a girl I know to be a local orphan in wrist chains and tears upon the ground." Jeremie made a move toward Ginny, but the man stopped him.

"This creature is of no use to you, but of great value to me."

"She is not property. No matter what you think of her, she is not yours to put on display for profit."

"I'm sorry, Prince, but I believe your father is the real ruler of this land. He carries all the weight, so they say, and you are just a product to cure a curse."

"Huh," Jeremie responded, stroking the tiny black stubble that peeked through his pale skin. "And what village may I ask are you from, to have all these knowledgeable opinions about my kingdom."

"Oh, I don't live here. I don't live anywhere. I am a man of the mountains, one who cannot be tied down."

"Well, in that case, you have traveled into this land without proper papers. No one comes here. Please unlock my friend and be gone from the kingdom of Inniskellin, as you are banned forever from trespassing within its lands."

"Fuck you, you can't do that."

"Oh yes I can." Jeremie hauled back his fist and slammed it into the side of the man's face. Lydia, who had been silent up till now, let out a cry.

"Guards!"

At his majesty's call, ten guards rattled down the stairs in their armor. How they had been so close and no one had heard them, Ginny would never know.

"Find the key and unlock her immediately," he said, pointing to the man who rolled about on the ground, possibly with a broken jaw. "Then escort him to his caravan and from this land forever," he paused. "As for you...," he began, turning toward Lydia.

"*Never!* I am never going back there." She anticipated sweet freedom, and now she couldn't bear to abandon that dream, even though now she would have no companion to travel with or to steal from. But she would come up with some way. She was a survivor. She scrambled to her feet and ran off of her own accord.

They didn't live in a time that was kind to young women out on their own. Ginny wondered what would become of her. But Ginny could say she would sleep better tonight with Lydia gone.

"Are you alright?" Jeremie addressed Ginny directly for the first time during their encounter, helping her up now that she was free from her bonds.

"Yes, I guess. Shaken up, mostly."

"I can understand. Should I have locked him up in the dungeon instead?"

"No, just keep him away from me."

"As you wish, my subject. I am here to serve you."

"Thank you, Jer— Your Majesty. I cannot ever begin to repay you for your kindness here today."

"Don't think anything else of it. I am glad I came when I did."

"I am glad you did too." Ginny looked at his hand, only to notice his knuckles were injured where they had come into contact with Chester's jaw. "Oh, you're bleeding. Please, let me dress it for you. It is the least I could do."

"No, no. There is a nurse inside for that. Are *you* alright? Do you need medical attention?"

"Oh no. I, I actually need to get back to my booth now. Miss Peters will be furious that I was gone this long."

"Maybe I could bring you by a bite to eat, to regain your strength."

Ginny thought of how the other girls and Miss Peters might react to such a gesture by him on her behalf. "No, no. That won't be necessary." Ginny turned and began to run up the stairs, as quickly as her clumsy, wide feet would allow.

"If you are sure there is nothing further I can do to be of assistance…"

"No, no. But… Thank you." She turned to him and they locked eyes. His were warm and friendly.

"I am at your service anytime, my lady."

Ginny giggled at the ridiculousness of that statement as she made her way back.

Miss Peters was angry that she had been gone so long. It was time to begin packing up. When Lydia never showed up for the wagon ride home, Miss Peters only ruminated that it was one less mouth to feed. Ginny was glad that she was gone, but knew that a void in the pack had been created. An existing girl, or the next one to show up on the doorstep, would no doubt step into the alpha bitch role. Even with all that had happened, Ginny rode home with a smile on her chapped lips. She had noticed that the prince had walked by their booth several times, as if to make sure that she still remained unharmed. That is what she would tell herself as she drifted off to sleep tonight.

The snow on top of the mountain peaks never melted anymore, creeping down lower every year when no one was looking, like a dog moving in on a full dinner plate. The winters in Inniskellin gradually grew colder. The summers became shorter. The curse continued to plague all living things: plant, animal, and human. Farmers had to sow as many seeds as they always did to have a tiny yield of produce.

Miss Peters had stopped taking in new girls years ago. As the last batch grew and left, Ginny, at eighteen years, stayed to care for Miss Peters and the farm. As the plague continued to spread through the animal kingdom, it killed the neighbor's horse they often borrowed. When it came time to head to market, Ginny carried two big baskets across her shoulders, hoping to be able to trade the few vegetables she had for some meat or possibly some medicine for Miss Peters. The sickness was taking its toll on the elderly population. There was no cure, but medicine could make her more comfortable.

Large booths had been replaced with tables, sometimes two or three families sharing one. When the king and the prince walked through, the king's expression was filled with gloom. His skin was an unhealthy gray. He looked the thinnest he had ever been. Jeremie's mood was not much better, until he spotted Ginny. She tried to give him a small smile, to lift his spirits. He managed a half smile for her and approached the table.

"Hey. So you had enough extra goods to bring to market?" he asked her.

"Not really. But we were sick of eating potatoes for every meal. We were hoping to get a little variety."

"But that's not the whole story, is it?" Jeremie said, looking accusingly at the amber bottle of medicine she had already obtained.

"No," Ginny replied shyly.

"You are not sick—" His dark brown eyes opened wider, concerned.

"No, no... But Miss Peters is."

Jeremie sighed. "All this death, and it is all my fault."

"No, it's not. It is the witch's fault for cursing us all in the first place."

"But I could end it all. If I could only find the most beautiful woman. We are having another line-up here at the castle next week. Be sure to tell your neighbors."

These events had been held regularly without any success. But the prince was so handsome that no one minded kissing him. And no one in authority had any better ideas.

"Of course I will," Ginny smiled brightly at the prince. Then, remembering what she must look like to him, she bowed her head. She was embarrassed at the way she always reacted to the prince. She could feel her giant nose getting red and her already ruddy cheeks getting redder.

"I will see you later, then."

"Sure, sure, Your Highness."

Suddenly his hand was under her chin. She jumped back, not used to any sort of human touch, except the cruelty inflicted by Lydia. But it had the desired effect. She was looking right at him now, even if she wore a look of shock.

"I told you before to call me Jeremie." He smiled once more and was gone. All Ginny could do was nod after him. How many times had he touched a girl like that before kissing her? Probably none of them had ever reacted as she had.

Ginny would love a chance to kiss the prince, but that would never happen. Everyone knew the curse called for him to kiss the most beautiful girl in the land. Everyone knew that Ginny did not fit that bill. And she knew that better than anyone.

It did not stop her cheeks from flaming bright red at the thought. She knew that would only make the white and black heads ripening from her pores stand out even more.

So much death.

Ginny had been holding on to Miss Peters's hand when she took her last breath. Ginny had been at her side the past twenty-four hours, ever since her breaths had begun to sound wet and labored. She had learned from a neighbor that it was a sure sign that her lungs were filing up with fluid and the end was near.

Ginny knew she had to get started digging the grave. She should have a month ago, but she didn't want Miss Peters to die alone. For the same reason, the cupboards were bare. Ginny was weak with hunger, but there was really nothing left of value to trade for food. Money was of no use any longer. It was worthless because people only wanted the goods. What good was a pile of coins when you were dying and needed medicine? The medicine man didn't want your money, he wanted food or candles or matches. Crops would no longer grow in the poisoned fields.

All she could do right now was go out to the porch, lie on her cot, and sleep until her energy was restored. She needed to distance herself from death, just for a short while.

Her sleep was interrupted by a party on horseback stopping purposely in front of the house. She supposed it was her house now, what was left of it anyway. She never thought that she would have her own house. She didn't have anything to pay the taxes with, but when the curse had taken a turn for the worst, the kingdom had stopped collecting taxes. And there was no one looking to swoop in and buy a derelict property. No one would dare travel to our land for fear of catching the curse.

She must have been out for only a few hours, but the nap had given her more energy. She rubbed the sleep from her eyes to see who it was, already knowing it could only be one person.

"Hey, Guinevere." Jeremie was the only person to call her by her full name. Really, there was no one else to ever call her name at all, now that Miss Peters had passed on. "Hope I haven't come at a bad time?"

"Actually, it is. Miss Peters has... passed on."

"Just today?"

"Yes, earlier. I still need to take care of the body." She motioned into the cottage. "I had to rest up a little first."

"Oh my. My deepest sympathies. Please allow me to assist in any way that I can."

"No, no Jeremie. I could never allow you to do that, especially now that you have been elevated to the positon of king."

"By a most unfortunate set of circumstances, much the same as you find yourself in, I'm afraid. Please let me help. It is the least I could do for all the hospitality you have shown me over the years. Do you realize this is the first time you actually called me by my name? Just now you did. And you haven't bowed, which I get so sick of. Please, let me do this for you."

Ginny grimaced, thinking how wonderful it would be for once to have help with back-breaking work. Hell, any help at all.

"Sir, do you need some of the men to assist?" a knight asked. He had been at Jeremie's right since they arrived. He obviously held the post of the new king's right-hand man. Even in her post-nap brain fog, she remembered his blond hair from a previous visit. Now it was longer than it should be for a man of royal service, shaggy hair over his ears and curling at the base of his neck. He wasn't any older than Jeremie himself.

"No Luke, that won't be necessary. I can handle this. Why don't you take the men down to the fork in the road at the end of the woods. Wait for me there."

"But Jeremie—"

He had used his familiar name. There must have been a friendship prior to the professional one.

"I got this. Just go." Jeremie didn't say it rudely, but it was received as the order that it was.

Luke nodded, unloading a couple of saddlebags from the horses, sitting them on the porch. Someone tied up Jeremie's horse to a nearby tree. It is good they didn't hitch it up to the porch post, because it was rotten and about to give way at any time. The men then mounted up and rode away, disappearing into the dead woods. Ginny and Jeremie watched as they departed. The fading hooves gave way to the sound of the nakid branches rubbing against one another in the breeze.

Ginny shifted on the tiny cot, causing it to creak. She braced her hands against the edge.

"I supposed I should get to this." She stood, and instantly pitched to the left. She closed her eyes and cringed in preparation for her head cracking on the splintered wooden planks. But something stopped her before she hit.

"Whoa, there?! When was the last time you had something to eat?" he asked.

"Um, I'm not sure. Wednesday?"

"Today is Wednesday."

"Oh. Then last Wednesday, maybe?"

His arms around her felt good. They were holding her up, but also holding her together somehow. Even a few weeks ago, she would have been embarrassed by this situation. But she was so exhausted. She couldn't right herself. His warm body pushed her back down to a sitting position. She gazed into his eyes, hoping it conveyed the thank you she was too frail to speak.

He dug through the saddlebags, taking out food and drink, handing it to her. She shoved a stick of jerky into her mouth and tried to bite it off, but it was exceptionally tough.

"Sorry. That's squirrel. It doesn't taste so bad, but it is chewier than beef. All the cows tipped over and died, but those damn squirrels are still everywhere. They may end up being the only survivors of the curse."

"Mmm. It's s'okay. The sauce on it tastes sweet and good," she mumbled feebly with a full mouth.

"Really? The chef made it incredibly weak."

"I'm not really used to sweets."

"That's a shame."

Ginny took a large gulp from Jeremie's silver canteen. Then she coughed loudly, red liquid running down her chin onto her clothes.

"Let me guess. You aren't used to wine either."

Ginny shook her head in response, wiping her mouth with the back of her hand.

"So many wells have gone bad that we cannot always trust the water to be potable. So we bring wine."

Jeremie handed her something round, white, and spongy. It smelled like cheese, but she had never seen so much of it in one serving before.

"Break some off. I don't want to take it all."

"It's no problem. We have more back at the castle. Eat."

She took a small bite, then a larger one. The hunger in her stomach persisted and she couldn't even taste the food as she consumed it. When she had made short work of the cheese, he handed her a hardtack biscuit. It had no real taste at all and a rather unpleasant texture, but her stomach finally stopped the sensation of trying to gnaw itself away. Jeremie gave her another, which she also gobbled. It was dry and she had to drink more of the wine to wash it down. She had never consumed alcohol in her life, but knew she could lose all the precious food she had consumed if she overdid it. After sitting a few more minutes, she stood again. She wobbled, but did not fall this time.

"Are you sure that you are up for this?"

"Better it be now than later."

They walked together out through the pasture, until Ginny showed him the spot. They began digging, finding a steady rhythm with one another as they moved the earth.

They sat on a log next to a fire in the yard as the sun sank and the moon rose, no one wanting to spend time in the room where Miss Peters's body had lain lifeless all day long. They caught two rabbits for dinner and cooked up a stew with some of the potatoes and carrots the king was given earlier in the day by other enamored citizens. They ate every last drop with the rest of the hardtack and the wine. Ginny now felt more full and content than she had at any time ever before in her lifetime. The warm fire felt good on her aching arms. Only a bath could feel better. She was so relaxed that her eyelids were getting heavy. She had begun to doze when Jeremie spoke.

"I don't know how you have done it all these years, Guinevere," Jeremie began. "My parents recently passed on, and now I know what an orphan must feel like. I have no one else in the world to call family."

She loved how he always used her full name. His voice had a lilt to it that she found pleasing, even though the topic was sad.

"Miss Peters was like a mother to me. An exceedingly strict one, but she made sure for nineteen years that I always had food when I was hungry and she cared for me when I was sick. She didn't say that she loved me, but it felt like her actions showed it."

"Have you ever had anyone else? A friend? Maybe another girl at the orphanage?"

"No. The other orphans were...um, cruel, but..."

"Why would anyone be cruel to you?" Jeremie asked.

"Oh, you know how children can be, especially with anything different." She felt like she had tried to get this same point across to him before.

"Why did you let them treat to you like that?"

"It is not like I could have stopped them. And I know what I am."

"And what are you?"

"If you are too blind to see it, I am not going to restore your sight."

He was too handsome for anyone to ever find fault with his appearance. And anyone who might attempt to tease or be cruel to him would simply be removed from the castle. He would never know what it would be like to have to share a bedroom, a dinner table, a bath, with those who hated you so much that they wanted you dead. All because they were beautiful, something you could never be, no matter how much you wished for it.

To get smarter, you studied your books and lessons. To learn music, you practiced your instrument until it was like a part of you. To farm, you watched what worked and what did not one year to the next, trial and error. But there was no cure for ugly.

Oh, people sold them. Ginny could still remember how traumatic her experience with makeup had been.

"I did have a friend for an awfully short time. We would play together when she came to visit her grandmother, Mrs. O'Brien, down the road. We used to pretend we were sisters. We would play in the forest where no one would see us. But one time her grandmother spotted us. The girl no longer came to visit."

Ginny was silent for a while. If he was going to ask her personal questions, it seemed only right that he should answer some of hers.

"Have you ever been in love?" She did not know where her boldness with the prince came from. Since he had helped her dig a grave and bury a dead body, there was nothing that was off limits anymore, despite their varying stations. Death had a way of equaling out all the disparities in their unlikely friendship.

"I wish I could say yes. I spend all this time kissing women, but most of them are only interested in marrying a prince, now a king. It can make a person lonely."

"That's sad... You know, you will never find your queen. You are going about things all wrong. If you wanted, I have a few suggestions."

"You? Like what?"

"You need organization. You need a current map of the kingdom, a grid system. You need everyone to register their birth with the kingdom. Systematically track who you have already kissed so that less time is wasted covering the same ground over and over and over."

"That sounds great! Wait—how long have you had these ideas?"

"A few years now," Ginny answered sheepishly.

"Why didn't you say something sooner!?"

"Who would listen to the ideas of a troll?" Ginny answered matter-of-factly.

"You are no troll. And tomorrow, you ride with me and my men. We begin on this organization plan of yours."

"Me? I can't travel with you. I am just a commoner."

"Why not? There is nothing left here for you."

Ginny looked around the ramshackle cabin and the dormitory that had collapsed in on itself. Jeremie was right. The kingdom's end was closing in on them all. The odds were stacked against her. She had nothing left to live for. So, by that reasoning, she also had nothing left to lose.

"Alright, I will ride with you."

"We will have to get you a horse," Jeremie said, thinking out loud.

"You really should get some rest, Your High— I mean Jeremie. Please, use the cabin. It is small, but you could use my bed. It is comfortable."

"Thank you. Your generosity and ideas shall be rewarded."

Jeremie went into the cabin and closed the door. Ginny wrapped herself up in a thick horse blanket and slept on the porch.

# I NEED YOUR ARMS

I need your arms
To hold me tight
To make me feel safe
And loved
For even just one night
I need your arms
To protect me
From the things I can't help
Thinking about
But somehow your arms
Soften their blow
I need your arms
To never let me go

It was a while later in the morning before they found the knights. Ginny had to walk until then, when a knight gave up a horse to her. It was that way when in the presence of a king. He got the best accommodations and transportation. No one thought anything more about it.

When people balked at the king's new travel companion, he quieted them with a most direct response.

"She can help, and she is my friend."

It didn't stop villagers from staring and pointing, but Jeremie's confidence in her did make her feel more worthwhile inside.

The royal party returned to the castle at dusk. Ginny was shocked at its appearance. The stones were chipped, the walls were cracked, and the drawbridge was disabled, stuck in its open position.

"It is not necessary to ever close it," Jeremie replied to her unspoken question, her mouth hanging open in surprise. "No other kingdoms dare to step foot in ours. They are afraid they would take the curse back home with them." He chuckled to himself. "It's not like it is lice. It is a witch's curse, for Christ's sake."

Once inside the castle walls, Ginny was separated from Jeremie and the rest of the guardsmen she had been traveling with. She was led by a handmaiden to a guest chamber all her own. Although a fire was prepared, the mostly empty room still felt damp and cold. As it was time to turn in for the night, she climbed into the bed and tried to sleep. It eluded her.

Ginny didn't know what was worse:

- Sleeping in a dorm with girls who may kill you in your sleep.

- With a dying Miss Peters in the same room.

- In an unfamiliar room deep in a cold castle all by yourself.

G inny soon grew accustomed to the routines of the castle. They still felt strange to her though: regular meal times, clean clothes, leisure time.

The plague had of course had an effect on the castle supplies, but a guest could request anything their heart desired and almost always receive it. It was different from how Ginny had grown up. What they had at the orphanage, Ginny had in large part worked to create. That was not the case here. She never even saw the people growing the food or making the quilts. Although the work on the farm was hard at times, Ginny had always found comfort in it. This life of leisure was somehow unfulfilling. She found it boring and empty. It was easy to see how someone could get spoiled living this lifestyle.

And being around to observe Jeremie more, it appeared that is just what had happened to him.

Although he had seemed heartfelt back at the cottage when he explained experiencing a whole new level of lonely now that his parents had both departed, he was still living the life of a king inside the castle. It somehow didn't sit right with her that those in his service in the kingdom were dying more every day, beyond these stone walls, while the king had all the wine and food he could eat.

And the women! Ginny's first dinner she attended in the castle, she ate at a long table with some of the other knights she had traveled back to the castle with. The king sat at the head of the table, of course. He had a voluptuous maiden on either side of him. They fawned over him, he whispering sweet nothings into their ears. The pair giggled so much it seemed they never had time to eat. Ginny observed that if they ate, they might pop the corsets on their frocks. Many of the guards did not hide that they were enjoying watching the four pale bosoms jiggle in delight. Luke was one of the few whose concentration was centered on his plate. That was the first day after they had returned.

The dinners after that, the king only had one girl at his side. But it was always someone different, always someone who would laugh while in his company. Ginny had to admit to herself that she was jealous of those lasses at first. But the jealousy grew into pity for Jeremie. Ginny had never had any real love in her life, but she assumed that Jeremie had from his parents, at least. Once you knew real love, how could you be happy gallivanting around with someone dimmer than a lantern with a filthy chimney?

Sleeping at night in the castle continued to be difficult. Ginny rather formed a habit of sneaking down to the massive library to read. She had her choice from thousands of great works of fiction, and non-fiction books on science and art. Most covers were made of ornate leather. Many were so old they had been copied down by hand in ink. Ginny felt it a shame that it was all locked up here in the castle. The kingdom would be much better served if it could be shared with them for the education and betterment of all.

This became such a custom that the handmaiden regularly started a fire in the room, anticipating Ginny's arrival. Ginny would stay and read until close to dawn, until her eyes burned and watered, her eyelids so heavy that she could no longer hold them up. On a few occasions, she even fell asleep on the chaise in the library. When she awoke and realized it was daylight outside, she rushed back to her room, so as not to be seen in her night robe.

Jeremie had the war room in the castle tidied up and turned into the headquarters for the new Curse Task Force. To begin with, it was Ginny and Jeremie, Luke, who she had come to realize was his closest friend and confidant, and the Secretary of War, Ned Bobkins. After a few days of Bobkins dismissing everything Ginny said as "rubbish," he was removed from the room, and she could only suspect from duty as well.

In Bobkin's absence, Ginny felt more comfortable expressing her ideas to Jeremie and Luke. When they did chuckle, they asked where she came up with such an idea. When she explained she got it from a book, they discussed it further to see if it could actually be implemented. They realized what Bobkins, old and set in the ways of the past—a peaceful time with unlimited resources—would never understand. The kingdom was desperate and running out of time. Although the king didn't live that way in his own castle, he had seen the decimation to his kingdom and its inhabitants.

Once the trio had outlined their plan, they brought in the other knights to share with them what they had built, many of the ideas new and original, coming from Ginny herself. The day before when Jeremie had told her she should be the first one to speak in front of all these people, she had thought he was joking. These were all combat-trained, skilled weapons handlers, and a roomful of men, none the less. She was just an orphan farmer with an insatiable reading habit.

In this kingdom, women ruled their own homes, giving orders to their husbands and sons. But out in the common areas, men were believed to rule. If only Ginny could simply dress as a man, as she had read a female warrior did in a story. But her deformed appearance would make her recognizable, no matter what she wore. Maybe the males had to project a strong front, possibly based on male posturing should any other countries consider invading. This was no longer necessary for Inniskellin. It was dead land. It was not desired by anyone, except those still trying to live off it. It was believed to be a lost cause by most, even the servants residing in the king's own castle.

Ginny stood up in front of the men in the room. She started sweating and shaking. She had read in books where some people did things like this as part of school. It was often referred to as "public speaking." But no one in Inniskellin had received that kind of education. Ginny had never done anything else like this in her entire life. She squeezed her eyes shut and sucked in a deep breath. As it escaped her body, so did the words she had rehearsed all night, so that she wouldn't sound like an idiot.

"We need to go about fighting this curse like a war, not as if it is some joke, going through the motions. We need to be tactical about our response." Ginny was silent, waiting for them to laugh and jeer her. She finally opened her eyes, but no one was laughing. No one was even smiling. They were... listening. Ginny had been so worried that she wouldn't be able to get her words out that she never thought about what would happened if she actually did. When she realized they were paying attention to her, she couldn't find a way to go on.

"Why don't you give them some of the highlights," Jeremie coaxed her.

She ripped her eyes off the roomful of men who were becoming more curious by the minute. She stared at the grain in the wood table in front of her as she began.

"The king has been searching for the maiden of prophecy for over a decade, with no success. This business of holding random line-ups here and there has had a zero percent success rate. It is time to make a strategic plan with measureable criteria." Ginny got stuck again. She ran her hand back and forth along the bark on the unfinished edge of the meeting table. She swore she heard a cricket chirping in the back corner of the room.

"The specific points," he urged.

"The specific points," she chose to begin with his words because they sounded official and right. "First, we will have the artists create a chart, a map, of Inniskellin. Then, we need to create a system to assign a number to each household. We will name main thoroughfares. Each resident's name will be logged. If they do not go by a surname, we will work with them to assign one. As someone is born, they will be added to our records. When someone dies, it will be noted. In this way, we can then create a grid system. We can cover each sector, know what women we have already interacted with," Ginny stopped again. That was everything she could think of at this moment, under the pressure.

"This will be tracked in official ledgers. Ginny, here, will be in charge of that. I know it sounds like it will take a lot of time, and it will. But that is why we need to get moving on all this immediately—today. And we will be able to tell where we have been, and where we need to keep searching. That concludes this meeting. We will be calling each of you in individually as the day goes on to go over your specific duties with you. You will be taking orders during this maneuver from either Luke, Ginny, or myself. I don't expect any of you to have an issue with this. Dismissed."

The men rose and filed out of the room. They talked amongst each other as they made their way out into the hallway, their boots echoing on the stones.

One knight, one of the youngest for sure at not much more than fifteen, bounced up and down on his heels as he left the room. He was thin with straight black hair, average in every way.

"I'm glad there is going to be another expedition. They told me I was too young to serve on the last one. Nobody is going to tell me that this time. I can't wait to get started."

"In the middle of the coldest, longest winter we have ever had? I am not that eager to go, Erik. You can have my place. I'll stay here in my nice castle chamber. You can report back and let me know all the fun you are having."

"Seriously, Cassian. This could be epic. I might not even mind taking orders from that thing." They moved further down the hallway, their voices evaporating into the distance.

She collapsed into her chair. Jeremie wrapped his arm around her and squeezed.

"You did great. Coming up with the plan is the hardest part. Hard part is over," Jeremie whispered the words of comfort right next to her ear.

It seemed impossible, but Ginny was actually growing accustomed to these simple gestures of affection. At first she had wanted to jump out of her skin when he made physical contact, a fear response. It still felt strange and unfamiliar now, but not necessarily wrong. She had realized in her time at the castle that Jeremie was this way with all who were close to him. Maybe that is how normal people were. She wouldn't know. Nothing about her upbringing had been normal.

Although it had been a trying day, and Ginny was exhausted, she still could not sleep. She found herself headed down the familiar stone passageways to the library. She carried a candle with her, but it only lit where she was. It didn't do much to illuminate the path ahead. As she rounded a corner, she heard voices. Or more correctly, giggling. And kissing. Ginny didn't realize until this exact moment that kissing even had a sound. She didn't know who could be down here. These rooms were more guest bedrooms, like her own. Usually they were quiet when she passed by this way. Another curve in the hallway blocked her view of who the voices belonged to. But when she heard the next words, she could identify one of them.

"I'll show you what a king's sword looks like."

Then a high peel of laughter. "I think I have a sheath that will fit that perfectly," the unidentified girl's raspy voice insinuated.

Jeremie's chuckle in response was deep and sexy. Something stirred deep within Ginny. Usually she was excited anytime she was in his presence, but this was—more. Her breath caught in her throat. She thought she had defeated the urge to be jealous of the king's conquests once and for all. But it all came burning back. She felt the heat crawl up her thick neck and up her disfigured face. Somehow it burned hottest in the scar on her cheek, the one Lydia had given her, a reaction to her own jealousy over the prince ignoring her. The same scar that, ironically, the prince had noticed on Ginny's face, despite all the other blotches and blemishes. The scar that made her realize he was really seeing her, and not all the ugliness attached to her.

The angry fire pushed her forward, needing to witness the scene with her own eyes. The heavy wooden door creaked, as they pushed it together, the hinges protesting. When they came into her sight, they were already in motion, headed into the room. Light from the fire, already lit by some poor handmaiden no doubt, leaked into the hallway, illuminating them. Their arms were entwined, his head buried into her long, red, curly hair, still laughing. It looked like an extension of the flickering fire within. Ginny kept moving, unable to stop herself. At the last moment, Jeremie raised his head out of her luscious locks to lock eyes with Ginny. The flame from her small candle reflected off of his piercing eyes in the near darkness. His smile changed when he spotted Ginny. If anything, he seemed curious why she was here. She fought the urge to grab him and pull him out of the room. Then they disappeared and the door shut with a slam.

Ginny doubled over in the hallway, dropping her candle, instantly snuffing it out. She pitched forward, both her hands catching her, now flat against the cold stone floor. The jealous rush left her so quickly, she felt sick at its absence. The emptiness felt as though a lung had been ripped out of her. That fast it had become part of her body, causing it to suffer in its absence. Who knows how long she may have stayed like that in the dark passage, the only light a small trickle coming from under the door of the solely occupied room, but she heard the sound of something scurrying alongside of her. She jumped up and turned back the way she had come, following the wall with her hand back to her own chamber. There she threw up, then cried herself to sleep.

The next day Ginny found it hard to concentrate as they tried to come up with names for the roads in the kingdom. Jeremie made no mention of what had happened the night before. Of course he sat there looking dashing as always, his jet black hair combed perfectly, wearing a jacket made of black leather, accentuating his dark eyes. He probably didn't even remember. She suspected he may have been inebriated. At least that is what she told herself to justify why he could sleep with a little harlot like that.

"Ginny, is that alright with you?"

Luke's voice broke into her silent brooding.

"What?"

"Do you agree we should name the road from the mill to the castle 'Mill Road?' " he repeated.

"Oh yes, that is fine with me," she replied unenthusiastically. She continued gazing down at the table in front of her.

"Just checking. You weren't happy we named the road to the castle Talbot Way," Jeremie snapped.

Ginny flung her head up to meet his glare. A fraction of the jealousy from last night rose up in her once again.

"I thought since it was made of cobblestones that 'Cobblestone Way' would be better suited for it. That is how I have always thought of it since I was a child."

"As I explained before, I felt it necessary to honor my father's memory. And the road to the castle is the most appropriate," he chided her.

"So, by that logic, the cow path that runs in front of the orphanage should be 'Dirty Orphan Lane?' " she replied hotly.

"Actually, I was thinking Peters Lane," he shot back.

"Oh," Ginny replied.

Luke watched as each one of them volleyed their words off the other. This must have in turn made Jeremie more conscious of how silly they were being.

"And I think I need to remind you who at this table *is* the king."

"Then maybe you should start acting more like one. I am doing all this to save your kingdom when all I want to do is let it get destroyed by the curse." Ginny got up quickly, her chair falling back onto the floor with a loud thwack. She hurried out the door. Instead of turning right to go back to her room, she ran left to head outside.

"What was that all about?" she heard Luke ask as she hurried down the hall.

She didn't want to be cooped up within the castle walls any longer, although the courtyard walls weren't much better. It had turned cold already. When she was young, Ginny could remember that winter wouldn't begin until November. Now it was early September. No wonder the fields never had a chance to produce plentiful crops anymore. Their growing season had been obscenely reduced.

Ginny wrapped her arms around herself, trying to stay warm. Her teeth began to chatter, letting clouds of white breath escape from between her lips. She no longer wore dresses made out of thin rags as she had at the orphanage. Being in the castle and part of the planning team had come with the benefit of quality garments. Of course, the proportions of Ginny's body didn't match any existing pattern or dress form, consequently clothes had to be custom made. She had gotten a long coat for weather such as this yesterday, but it was in her chamber. In her haste of emotional distress, she hadn't taken the time to return to her room to fetch it. She hated the thought that at the height of harsh winter, the men would be setting out on their last ditch effort to save the kingdom. The speed at which the environment was deteriorating now, they likely had less than a year before all the kingdom would be wiped from its newly-created maps. At least that is what the best minds at the castle estimated. As Ginny surveyed the skeletal trees against the brown of the hills leading to the mountains, she could only concur.

Suddenly her back and shoulders were enveloped in a warm cocoon, instantly making her muscles relax, not even realizing before that they had been tensed with chill.

"You must be freezing out here," Jeremie commented.

She pulled the jacket tighter around her chest, trying to preserve his body heat that had been dispensed with the garment.

"I am. Thanks," she said, looking up to meet his eyes, meaning to convey only gratitude, but then she found she couldn't look away. Jeremie was the first to break the hold. He surveyed the land in front of them.

"Not much of a view here."

"Maybe I needed to be reminded of what we are working for," Ginny stated.

"In that case, I wish you could have seen this view a decade ago, when it was filled with green grass and a rainbow of blooming flowers," he mused.

"It must have been beautiful."

"It was."

"Maybe you should have kissed it," Ginny said, then looked sideways at him, a smirk on her face.

"Ha, ha. You are so funny," he smiled, playfully bumping her shoulder with his own. His arms were now wrapped around his torso, attempting to fight off the cold. "I thought it was September," he frowned.

"It is."

"I guess we should move up our time table then."

"I suppose so." Jeremie placed his arm around her shoulders.

"C'mon. Lunch is probably ready."

They walked back through the stone arch together, into the castle.

inny was surprised to find that the next time she looked at the progress made on the map of roadways Luke and Jeremie had been working on it in her absence. Her eyes were drawn to a road that had been crossed out and renamed. One of the main roads away from the castle, one that actually forked off of Talbot Way, was now named Guinevere. It didn't have a lane or street after it, only her name. Tears came to her eyes as she kept reading it over and over again to make sure she wasn't imagining it.

She felt the presence of someone else behind her and turned to find Jeremie in the doorway. He was leaning casually against the door casing and was smiling because he knew exactly what she was looking at.

"Something special, for you."

"Thank you. But I don't deserve the honor."

"Oh, think of it as your Winter Holiday gift."

"But I have nothing to give you in return," she pleaded, her eyes locking with his brown eyes and losing herself in them a little.

"Oh, we'll see about that." He winked at her.

She smiled, careful to hide her teeth.

Ginny shook the silly teenage lovesick girl thoughts out of her head. She would be twenty next summer after all, an old maid by today's standards, as she would always be. She might as well find a way to be of service to the king.

Plus, she had her own personal rules to keep her out of trouble. Mental rules she recited in her head before she fell asleep at night so that she wouldn't forget them, rules to keep the walls up around her heart to prevent anyone from ever breaking it. Mostly, the walls crumbled at the most inopportune times. The list had been longer when she was at the orphanage. Over the years, they had all faded away but one:

*Don't* ever *believe for one minute that there is anyone who gives a damn about you—whether you are alive or dead, happy or sad—because they don't!*

It had served her well for many years. Some would say it was pessimistic. Some would say it was giving up. But Ginny only implemented it as a form of self-preservation.

**G**inny tried to ignore what Jeremie had said about the holiday approaching. They had never done much to celebrate at the orphanage. The girls had usually given each other gifts that they had handmade from whatever had been lying around. Knitted scarves or socks were popular. Ginny never received anything, subsequently it wasn't a big deal to her. Sure, she felt a pang of emptiness in her heart as the other girls exchanged presents and hugged each other, excluding her. But she was actually grateful; it was the one day annually that they never were outright cruel to her. If that was their gift to her, she would take it in a heartbeat. Would've been nice if it could last two days, or three, or a week though.

But apparently Winter Holiday was a much bigger affair at the castle. Jeremie kept assuring her that this year would be a small celebration, nothing like when he was a boy and his father had still been alive. He told her of how there had been visitors from foreign lands, including singers and dancers. They would perform at the great dances that were held in the castle's main ballroom. Ginny had accidentally walked into the empty space once when she had gotten lost upon first arriving at the castle. The room was ginormous. It was bigger than Miss Peters's cottage, the bed house, and the barn—combined. Jeremie assured her that it used to be filled to the brim with tables jam-packed with every delectable food you could think of (which Ginny could only think of two) and guests suited in their most elegant attire. She could not imagine it. And being an avid reader, she was usually good at utilizing her imagination.

Ginny was in awe of all the decorations that adorned the castle. Green boughs hung in the main hallways, the ones to and from the dining hall and the royal chambers. She had lost count of the number of pine trees that had been chopped down, brought inside, and decorated. The baubles and tinsel were so plentiful as to conceal any branch imperfections brought about by the plague. One ornament on any given tree looked like it was worth more than the orphanage had taken in in any single year. Ginny couldn't help but imagine if the girls from the orphanage ever got in here. They would be picking the trees bare of all their trinkets, not really caring about them, only what value they would have for resale.

On the last night of the Winter Holiday celebration, local musicians were brought into the castle to perform. There was a modest buffet of food for the intimate collection of guests. Ginny was curious, but she knew her place, knew that she did not fit in with that crowd. But she desperately wanted to listen to the music, and maybe a little of the voices of everyone else's merry-making. Accordingly, she hid in the library, with the door slightly ajar. She had a book in her lap, but found that her attention was not in it. She had been on the same page for over an hour, her eyes trailing over the same words but not comprehending them. Her concentration was with all the festivities nearby.

She jumped when the heavy wooden door groaned with movement.

"So this is where you are hiding yourself. You know, I almost had to send Luke out in the snow to search for you."

"You know I get cold easily. It is unlikely I would run off out in the weather."

"It wouldn't be the first time."

"That's true," she bowed her head, pretending to study her book.

"Why aren't you attending the party?"

"It would make me uncomfortable." It was the truth, and with a nod of his head Jeremie seemed to accept her answer. "I am enjoying the music though. I have heard so little in my lifetime. This is a rare pleasure."

"Well, we will have to see about getting more of it into your life."

They were both quiet for a moment. Jeremie moved to take a seat in the chair next to the settee Ginny was stretched out on. He leaned his head way back and exhaled, as if entertaining guests was an effort for him. Then he sat back up and met her eyes.

"I was hoping I could catch up with you before you turned in for the night."

"Why?"

"I have a present for you."

"Why? No, I don't need it. Your taking me into the castle is gift enough."

"You make it sound like the castle is another orphanage. From the few stories you have told me, I think I am insulted by that."

"Well, I didn't have anywhere else to go."

"You are not free-loading. You are here because you are contributing to the Curse Task Force. And you are doing an excellent job. And—and that is why I want to give you this," he stuttered thoughtfully.

He reached into an inner pocket of his coat and pulled out a small leather sheath. When he held it out to her, the light from the fireplace caught the silver in the handle and she had a loud intake of breath. She found herself reaching for it even as she said, "But I couldn't..."

"My father gave this to me when I was a boy. I mostly used it to whittle wood and stab scarecrows. But I've had it cleaned and sharpened, therefore it should be in excellent condition for you to take with you on the road."

"You mean I will be traveling with the company?" Ginny was dumbfounded. She had never expected this.

"Of course. I need my number one girl with me."

Her heart fluttered, although she knew he didn't mean it. Not in the way she wanted. Even then, even if someday he grew to like her as she did him, it was all for naught. Ginny knew she could never even allow herself to dream of one day marrying a king. The people of the kingdom would never allow it. Not that there was likely to be any kingdom left whatsoever.

"But you will need it for protection," she argued.

"I will have my sword, and several knights protecting me. But on the occasion you may get separated, it would be wise for you to have your own weapon."

Ginny relented and slid the knife from the sheath to examine it. She tried it out, stabbing the air in front of her. It was the perfect size for her chubby, female hands. "Alright. But when the mission is done, you must let me return it."

"I would never think of letting you do any such thing," he snickered.

Ginny smiled wide in spite of herself. But her head was bowed, so he couldn't tell, she didn't think.

She reached into a fold of her dress and pulled out a small book, handing it to Jeremie.

"What is this?" he asked, studying the plain brown leather cover.

"A gift. I uncovered it in the library."

"If it came from the library, then it is already sort of mine, isn't it?" he chuckled, looking at her sideways.

"But you would never think to go in there and poke around yourself. You needed me to find it for you," she smirked, knowing she had him. "Plus, what do you get the king who already has everything?"

"OK, I give. What is this?"

"It appears to be a history of the kingdom that Merrick kept on his own. I found it in a bureau drawer, almost as if someone was trying to hide it."

"Weird. So, it mentions my father a lot?"

"I only peeked, but it has your grandfather too."

He shifted it from one palm to the other, as if weighing the information contained within.

"Thank you for this. And for your friendship."

"Thank you. Blessed solstice to you."

"The same to you."

Despite his best efforts to avoid him, Erik had cornered Luke in the war room. They could not have been more opposite; Luke standing still, his right hand resting on the handle of his sword as had become habit, while Erik jumped up and down, his face ripening red like a tomato on the vine.

"First she gets to sit at the head table and tell the men what to do. Now she will be going on the expedition while I am left behind here? That is total bullshit, man. You have to get me in."

"I'm sorry, Erik. The king's decision on this matter is final," Luke replied, unmoved by Erik's plea.

"Those guys going are my friends. They see this as a betrayal to me and a misstep by the king. They will not stand for this. It will create a rift in the ranks," he gloated.

"You fancy yourself pretty important, don't you?"

"I do."

"Well, it won't mean shit when we are all dead. So keep your mouth shut and do your job," Luke spat. He couldn't help but catch the surprise on Erik's face as it registered that statement. Luke turned and left the room. It was his job to triple-check that the appropriate supplies had been gathered and packed according to orders. Unlike some people, Luke took his job seriously.

They set out in late January. At first, they visited all the houses in the shadow of the castle, thus they were able to return home at night. But this soon became impossible, as each day took them farther out to meet more people. With the supply wagons weighed down with food for man and beast, they set off on their extended journey in hopes of finding the right girl in time.

Ginny was in charge of the ledgers and maps. She recorded every villager they interacted with along the way. She had a different posture for official business. She stood up straighter, and she was more confident. She didn't doubt her thoughts and ideas; at least not until she had time to review them at the end of the day, when sleep escaped her.

Ginny never pictured herself the public relations type. But she was surprised to find that she was good at it. Once she opened her mouth and conversed with them on a personal level, the villagers believed her to be more intelligent than when she remained silent. When she helped them or answered their questions, they would smile welcomingly at her. She sometimes lost herself in the work and was able to forget she was a hideous freak. It made her feel good about herself, for a little while, anyway. This was a taste of what she imagined it felt like to be pretty.

Ginny's life finally had a greater purpose, which brought her a feeling of self-worth. The satisfaction she attained was by doing work that was traditionally for men, instead of fetching a handsome husband or raising a brood of rosy-cheeked children, as a typical woman was expected to.

While on the road in such close quarters with the king day after day, she could not always keep her thoughts in check. Sometimes Ginny imagined what it would be like to kiss the king. She knew such silliness would only lead to heartache, but she still could not help herself. Jeremie was of average height for a man. She would have been an average height for a woman, if not for her hunchback. She knew she would have to stretch up, and he would have to bend down to kiss her. When they stood next to each other, Ginny would secretly look at Jeremie's lips and imagine how they would feel against her own. Sometimes, while Ginny was daydreaming, she imagined herself taller, being able to simply close the distance between them and kiss him.

Ginny wore pants on the road, for warmth and to better mount and dismount her horse. She usually needed assistance from another guard, as her short legs and hump made it difficult. Luke usually did the task if he was nearby, or a few other kind-hearted guards. Some still refused to talk to her or be in her presence. Luckily Jeremie did not notice this, or he would have reprimanded them. Ginny didn't mind. She had expected people's reactions to her to be much more extreme. And, well, Jeremie was too busy to notice much of anything. He spent all day kissing women paraded in front of him, young and old alike, teeth or no teeth. But it was a young one he often kept around to spend the night with him. They would escape into a cottage he had commandeered for the night, the regular occupants hold up with their neighbors. The guardsmen had tents they slept in. Ginny usually stayed up late planning where they would travel the next few days. She would be by herself with a lantern and her paperwork in the supply tent. She would fall asleep there under several horse blankets, trying to preserve as much body heat as possible in the frigid night.

The unrelenting winter finally eased at the beginning of June. The conditions had slowed the party's progress more than they had anticipated. They had finished all but the farthest quarter of the kingdom, the Outlands. The orphanage had once marked the beginning of the Outlands. Ginny knew it would be a hard day when they finally traveled past the only home she had ever known.

Now that they were here, she could see that the cottage and barn had joined the dormitory in becoming nothing more than a pile of rubble. The green fuzzy moss had overtaken them, then the plague had killed it, turning it into nothing more than a brown and lifeless unrecognizable heap. It broke a piece of her heart that she didn't even realize was still whole enough to be broken. The entire party stopped there to rest for lunch. Ginny knew they were already a day behind by the latest schedule. But she wanted to go visit Miss Peters's grave.

"May I walk you to her grave?" Jeremie offered.

"No, no. I think this is something I best do on my own."

Ginny collapsed on the ground when she found the rocks they had placed on the mound of dirt that day ten months ago. She sat there and cried for a long time. When she was able to pull herself together, she talked to the stones, told them all about her new life with the king. She was more open with the Miss Peters of the afterlife than she would have ever been with the flesh and blood woman. Miss Peters was quick to judge, and even quicker with a switch. But Ginny wanted to share with someone the crazy turn of events her life had taken.

Ginny knew this would most likely be the last time she ever traveled this way again. They had yet to find the most beautiful girl, and Jeremie was running out of lips to kiss. Maybe the witch had lied to them after all, and there had never actually been a way to break it. Maybe it was all destined to fade out until there was nothing left of Inniskellin but an old legend.

Ginny made her way slowly back to the temporary encampment. She had just enough time to eat a bowl of vegetable stew before they packed up and rode out.

The Outlands could be dangerous. Despite their land being cursed, outlaws and criminals from other kingdoms hid in the Outlands, knowing the torture and imprisonments they would suffer in their own land could be worse than death. A dislocated criminal would have no respect for a king's traveling caravan. In fact, they would essentially have targets painted on their backs.

Jeremie reminded her to use the dagger she strapped onto her hip daily if she needed to. He said as she was the only woman in their party, she would be viewed as the weakest. Ginny wasn't as concerned. She was pretty sure a troupe of strangers, no matter how tough, would turn tail at the sight of her. They probably would not even realize that she was a woman as she was lacking a dress. More than likely, strangers would react to her with the same suspicion as the other guards had.

The party agreed to travel to the next inhabitable dwelling, allowing for the king to have a proper slumber. But nightfall was already upon them with no house in sight. A rider at the front carried a lantern, and also the rider at the back. That is when it happened.

The horses at the front fell, causing an awful noise and commotion that caused the steeds following behind to buck and jump. Ginny almost fell, regripping her reins so tightly that her fingernails dug into her own fleshy palms. She could hear shouting and swords being drawn all around her, the scraping of metal against metal that always foreshadowed death. The front lantern had broken and gone dark when the horse went down. The rear rider waved his light around wildly, trying to see what the threat was. Ginny caught sight out of the corner of her eye that Luke was positioning himself to protect Jeremie. Ginny quickly did the same. In the minimal flickering light, it looked as though there were four highwaymen trying to rob them. Two guards protected the ration wagon, but a robber made off with a box of food anyway. One tried to jump onto Ginny's horse to reach the king, but she promptly unholstered her dagger and jammed it through his hand. It stopped when it hit the tough hide of the horse, but the animal still whinnied and bucked, knocking the assailant to the ground. Ginny had to think fast to retrieve her blade in time. By the sickening crack and the man's shouting, she quickly surmised that the horse had trampled him.

Ginny would never know where the instinct to protect Jeremie had come from or the bravery to stop the criminal. She had only ever protected herself, and usually failed. She was not strong in body or mind. But a survival instinct had kicked in. She had been more than she knew she ever could be.

"Your Majesty, are you hurt?" Luke asked, distressed.

"No. I'm fine," Jeremie replied, his voice shaking.

"Everyone, jump on a horse. Cassian, take the lamp out front. Giddy-up!" Luke commanded. While Ginny was unsure what to do to make her horse go faster, he took off in time with the others. Two more curves, and they came upon a tiny cabin with smoke coming out the chimney.

The owners were excited to find the king at their door, and the king was even more excited to find the family residing in the house included five daughters. Ginny already knew this from her notes. The tents were hastily erected. The king would take the cottage for the evening. Ginny was carrying a box from the wagon into the supply tent when she saw Jeremie with the oldest daughter, headed inside the modest structure.

Ginny thought she was hidden in the cover of night, but there must have been enough backlighting from the fire that he spotted her unmistakable form. He raised his hand that was behind the daughter and gave Ginny a little wave. The daughter never saw it. Ginny kept moving into the tent, never acknowledging Jeremie.

It was probably about half an hour later when Ginny heard yelling coming from the cottage. She knew the king couldn't be in any danger, as Luke always slept right outside, guarding the door. But it peaked her curiosity, leading her outside to investigate. The door to the cabin flung open. She could just make out Luke standing sentry next to it.

"You are not at all like I thought. I always heard you were a sure thing," the girl yelled at him, pulling the collar of her dress up over her shoulder. Ginny could hear the pout in her voice.

"Well, you heard wrong. I'm not in the mood tonight."

"You bastard!" she screamed at him. She began to charge in the direction of the tents, the fire, and Ginny. Ginny ducked behind a tree.

"I could have you arrested for that. I am still the king!" he yelled, more sad than angry.

"You just try that. My dad has a sword twice as big as yours!"

Why did everything always end up being about the size of one's sword?

The girl ran past Ginny, unbeknownst to her, as Jeremie waved his hand at the daughter in the dark, shooing her away as one would a horsefly. He went back inside, leaving Luke to close the door behind him.

Ginny returned to her tent, trying to process what she had just seen. Why did Jeremie throw her out? Had he ever done that to any other women? She certainly appeared pretty enough, and willing. Why would he have turned that down?

As Ginny was still pondering all that, she doused her lantern to turn in for the night. A moment later, a shadowy figure entered her tent. She gasped in surprise.

"Relax. It's only me," Luke's calm voice clearly sounded to her ears in the small space. "I know you fancy yourself the lady of this tent, but I just don't feel right leaving a female unattended in these parts of the lands," he finished.

She laughed in spite of herself. The thought that she would ever be lady of *anything* she still found preposterous. But in this case, it was sort of true.

"Sure. Thank you," she responded once she had composed herself.

"I posted Cassian at the king's door. He will be fine," he continued, anticipating her next question.

"Oh," Ginny replied.

There was silence for several minutes. Ginny thought Luke had fallen asleep, but he had not.

"I was surprised that you wanted to accompany the king on this journey," he began.

"Why? Because I am a woman?"

"Not at all. Because it is cold and rough and thankless. If the king succeeds, we will never be a part of the legend; we are just the details. And you could have died for that tonight."

"We are all going to die soon anyway," Ginny responded diplomatically.

"I think it is more than that."

"Why are you out here, then?"

"Oh, well, I never had much of a choice."

"Why is that?"

"It was my birthright. You see, my father was the lead knight for King Talbot. Thus it is only proper that I should take the same post for his son, if I had the needed skills, which I do."

"Way to toot your own horn. So, wait. Your father was Merrick?"

Luke nodded. "I'm Lucas Merrick, at your service. Did you know my father?"

"The first time the king stopped by the orphanage, Merrick was with him."

"My father passed a few weeks before King Talbot did. The doctor said it was only a cold, said he would be well in a week's time. But, we buried him instead."

"I'm sorry."

"It's not like it was a big surprise. We all know our sentence."

"So, that is the only reason you are out here? Your duty to service?"

"No. I don't believe that would ever be a strong enough reason for me to do this job."

"Then why?"

"Jeremie and I were raised together. He has been my best friend for as long as I can remember, like a brother in many ways. For that reason, it makes it natural for me to want to protect his life."

"Do you think he would do the same for you?"

"He is. He is trying to do that for everyone in the kingdom."

With that, they both lay silently, a tall stack of crates between them, until sleep overcame them.

After that night, all the king's guards treated her as an equal. At first she could not understand the change. They explained it was because she had put her own life on the line to protect the king when danger threatened. They had all gone through years of training to be in his service. Ginny had done none of that. She was inexperienced with her knife, and she was a woman. Yet she had protected the king from injury and potentially saved his life.

Ginny was overwhelmed with emotion. They were saying that she belonged among them. She had never belonged anywhere, not even in her own mother's arms. None of them treated her differently now. They all slept in the same tent together. Miss Peters had always warned her charges about the dangers of being alone with a man, probably to prevent more unwanted babies at the orphanage. She never mentioned being alone with twenty of them! But they didn't see her as a woman, which was probably easy to do with her looks. They saw her as an equal. She was one of them.

She stayed on alert, just in case something in their moods was to suddenly change, to revert back to how they saw her before. Maybe they didn't really accept her, maybe they had just forgotten that she was there.

The posse rode their horses through the dark woods. More light was progressively entering their path as the towering trees began to thin. At the edge of the woods, they would find the village of Columbia Creek, as was labeled on the map they carried with them. The newly-minted mapmakers had been charting the kingdom ahead of them. It was long days for all those working on the Curse Task Force. No matter where they happened to be in Inniskellin today, they were fighting time, trying to find the girl who would be the cure before it was too late. More people died every day, including their own loved ones. Quite possibly, the most beautiful girl they were in search of as well.

They would be losing the daylight. There would only be time to find quarters for the night and have a meal. The sounds of the horses' hooves were slow and uneven. They echoed the exhaustion of their riders.

But as they got closer to the dimming light ahead, they could hear music. As they approached, it not only became louder, but they could hear laughter as well. When they broke through the trees, Ginny stopped her horse and stared in disbelief.

There were colored flags flying and the heavy smell of food hung in the air. There were jugglers and acrobats roaming about. Musicians played instruments Ginny had never seen before. Big boxes that folded up, then expanded again, and hollow wooden boxes with strings that made beautiful sounds. Some men blew through shiny metal horns they pressed to their lips.

"What's the problem, Guinevere? Haven't you ever seen a faire before?" Jeremie chuckled at her reaction.

"No," she relayed, still staring wide-eyed.

"What! Really? You have never been to a faire?" he said in disbelief. He stayed next to Ginny as the knights moved their horses past them, eager to check out the festivities. They all had smiles on their faces and were chuckling to one another. Ginny heard one of them saying he could not wait to drink a beer. Or five. Luke was the only one who lingered with them.

"There used to be festivals and faires all the time, for every season, for every reason, in every village. And the king would have them twice a year, to coincide with the royal balls. I thought all the villages had given up on having anything to celebrate. This is beautiful." He motioned his left hand in front of him toward the spectacle, his right hand still holding the reins.

The last few miles all the houses had been empty. They had begun to fear that the residents had all perished. But it was more likely now, upon discovering this sea of joy and merriment that they must all be here.

"There was no village near us to have a festival. The neighbors always went to the celebration in the next town. Miss Peters said we did not have the resources to go eat and play at the faire. Even when some of the girls grew up and went on their own, Miss Peters would keep me behind."

"But why would she do that? Was it a punishment?" Jeremie asked.

"No. Think about it. It would have been crueler to let me go."

"But I don't understand—"

"I know how it would have been. Everyone staring at the ugly freak."

"Oh, right," he answered, reluctantly.

"But it never stopped me from wanting to go. I would look at pictures in books and try to imagine what it would be like if it was real, and not flat on a page."

"And now that you are here, what do you think?"

"It is better than I could have ever imagined. Maybe this is just a dream, a figment of our imagination, like an oasis appears to a thirsty man in the dessert," Ginny said, speaking her thoughts out loud.

"Maybe. It definitely would not be a nightmare."

"Oh look!" she pointed. "They have rides! They look so exotic and fun."

"Then we shall ride them."

"What, oh no. It would probably be best if I stayed in for the night. Look, people are already starting to stare and point." Ginny instinctively tried to slouch down and hide, although presently she was still sitting high upon her steed.

"My dear girl! How self-centered you are? Don't you think it is possible that their attention is drawn this way because I am their king?"

"Oops. Sorry. Sometimes I forget that you are king. You are just, well, Jeremie to me."

He let out a long, loud laugh. "As it should be, my dear Guinevere. As it should be. C'mon."

He dismounted his horse. Ginny began to do the same. Jeremie reached his hands up to her waist and guided her down. She turned to face him and looked up to meet his eyes and thank him, but the words became trapped in her throat. All she could do was look into his dark brown eyes. They held her and she didn't know how to break free. He looked back at her.

"What?" he asked.

And the spell of his eyes was broken. Ginny bowed her head, ashamed. She knew her overinflated cheeks must be afire with color.

"I'm just nervous," she covered quickly. "I've never been to a faire before."

"Then hurry. Let's see what it has to offer, shall we?" He wrapped his hand around her upper arm and towed her along beside him.

Together they enjoyed all the pleasures the faire had to offer. They rode the rides. One was a big wooden wheel with benches hanging from it. Heavy ropes were wrapped around the center of the wheel, and then tied to a harness on a horse. When the horse pulled, it took them up into the air and back down again. Ginny held on tighter than was appropriate to Jeremie to keep from falling off as it jolted around. He kept his arm around her for the same reason. When they reached the end of the rope, everyone got off, and then the rope was rewound in the center again in preparation for the next ride. There was another that operated in the same general fashion, but it went around horizontal to the ground. They both laughed uncontrollably. Ginny was relieved that they had not eaten first. She feared all the delicious food would have come back out again.

They ate meat roasted on sticks over fires. They had rabbit, duck, chicken, beef— Oh, how long it had been since she had eaten beef! The last known cow had died in Inniskellin a year ago. Even Jeremie marveled at how long a side of beef in cold storage could last.

They began to walk around again and look at the various booths, talking with the local residents and those who traveled with the festival, a dying profession. Jeremie insisted that she hang onto his arm so that she did not fall behind and Luke could better shadow them, along with the other three knights that were on their left front, rear left, and rear right, respectively. As they walked, people tried to stop them, but Luke shooed them away if they tried to hold up the king for any more than a polite greeting.

With his attention on the king, Luke didn't realize when a woman approached Ginny, holding something out to her in her hand. She wore a hood over her head although her face could plainly be seen, one lock of white hair escaping from it. Ginny couldn't help but think she was about the age her mother would be if she had one. Despite all of Miss Peters's assurances, Ginny still suspected she was a troll hatched from an egg or something. Luke tried to push the stranger back, but she appeared friendly and bore a warm smile, therefore Ginny put a hand on Luke's arm to stop him from dismissing her. The woman opened her hand, letting a stone dangle from it on a silver chain.

Not knowing what the woman wanted, Ginny complimented, "It's beautiful."

The woman said something, but her voice was too quiet for Ginny to hear. "For you," she repeated, slightly louder.

"Oh no, I couldn't. But thank you anyway."

"For you," she insisted, not angry, still smiling.

"But—"

"If she wants you to have it, just take it," Jeremie said, leaning close to her ear. Ginny had not realized they had all stopped with her, and were listening to the exchange. Jeremie began to pull her along again, obviously not wanting to wait while she and the woman played hot potato with a piece of jewelry.

Ginny opened her hand then and let the woman place the object into it. Jeremie towed her away so quickly that she never gave a proper thank you, only waved to the woman as they continued on. She no longer noticed the sights and sounds nearby, her attention momentarily stolen by this gift. It was a blue stone polished to a brilliant shine. It was wrapped with a wire, then hung off of a long silver chain. She didn't understand how anyone could give someone else something so beautiful. Ginny had never owned a piece of jewelry in her life. It was an extravagance not many common folk bothered with. Food and clothes and livestock and seeds were the only necessities on most of the villagers shopping lists.

Jeremie had been cavalier about her accepting it. But he would be, wouldn't he? He had grown up as royalty. He was used to those with less always gifting him. Ginny couldn't even imagine that. It seemed backwards to her. Even as they had traveled, those with barely any food in their cupboards and their stomachs had given them nourishment along the way, when the royal party had brought all they needed along with them. And Jeremie had always accepted it without hesitation. It had been that way when she was a little girl and the king had first visited the orphanage. It was unethical.

And why had the woman given the necklace to her? Ginny was no one. The woman had obviously misunderstood her relationship with the king, thinking she was a member of the royal court when she was not. But the woman had insisted she take it. It appeared valuable. Ginny once again doubted that she should be in possession of such an item, but when she looked around, she saw no sign of the woman. She slipped it over her head so as not to lose it until she could locate the woman again to explain and return it. Ginny was thankful that the chain was extra-long to fit over her oversized head.

As they walked on, they saw a woman sitting under a canopy that read "Fortunes Told" who looked like she had fallen off a pirate ship and into Inniskellin. She sounded that way too.

"I suppose the curse has hurt your business greatly," Jeremie said as he approached.

"Aye, you could say that. Once the future held such promise, and was a booming business. Now, I don't look that far. I keep it all into the next few months, that is all."

"Well, would you do me the honor of reading my future?"

"Of course, Your Majesty. I am Lola. It is a pleasure to meet you."

Jeremie sat down in the chair across the table from her. He placed his hand into hers, which she grabbed up as if she had been doing this for decades, which by the look of her she had.

Wrinkles were such a part of her face, so deeply carved into her skin, that Ginny thought it must have looked empty in her youth with their absence.

"Let me see what our great king has in store for us."

She closed her eyes and was still. Jeremie closed his as well. After a couple of minutes, Ginny really wanted to poke the psychic to check to see if she was still alive. But then she began to hum. It was very low, so low that Ginny wasn't sure at first it was coming from her. She thought for a moment it must be from an insect, perhaps a honey bee. But the only ones still in existence were in the hive in the royal gardens. It did not pass anyone's notice what a dire circumstance that was.

"You will continue on your long journey," she began.

"I figured that much."

"You may think you are the mighty king, but don't mock the fates, aye."

At that, Jeremie's eyes popped open in surprise. Ginny would bet that not even his own mother had ever talked to him that way before. Maybe it would have done him a modicum of good if she had.

"You will meet many women, you will kiss them all."

"But will I find the one?"

"It would hurt me to look that far into the future."

"So that is a 'no.'"

"I would not presume to predict the fate of the entire kingdom. It looks as though your days will grow darker still."

"Ya, less sunlight, wonky seasons, I know this..."

"I do not mean physically, I mean mentally your days will grow dark. You will find it difficult to continue down the road to a resolution."

He pulled his hand away then. He rubbed it with his other hand, as if it was now sore. He got up quickly, and began to leave, before he turned back to pay her with food rations.

"I wondered if I could get a reading too?" Ginny was unaccustomed to asking for the things she wanted. Her voice was soft. They didn't act as though they had heard her at first. Then Jeremie motioned for her to take the chair he had vacated. She took the seat, his lingering body heat soothing her.

The psychic took her hand just as she had Jeremie's. Ginny closed her eyes, and then decided she didn't like that sensation. People were walking by them constantly, mingling about the faire and staring with curious eyes. She was afraid if she kept them closed, the villagers might begin to point at her and laugh. Old anxieties were hard to break. Consequently, she watched as the psychic's face grew pained at whatever she was seeing.

"You will continue this journey, accompanying the king. You will be a great comfort to him. You will return to the castle. But you will not find contentment there." She began to shake her head from side to side in dismay. "No, no. I don't want to see this. It hurts. It hurts."

Lola released Ginny's hand, opening her eyes. She rubbed her temples. Ginny sat there staring at her, waiting for a reply. Jeremie was not that patient.

"So, what did you see?"

Lola looked into Ginny's face. It was weird. It was not like she was looking at her, it was like the psychic saw *inside* of her somehow.

"It was very bright, a blinding light. And there was this feeling of beautiful love. But then there was this horrible anger. I've never experienced anything like it," Lola purred in her exotic accent.

Ginny stood. Lola studied Ginny and Jeremie standing next to each other. She waved her hand back and forth in front of them. "You two, you stick together. I think that would be best for everyone."

"Thanks for the advice. C'mon, Guinevere. Let's go," Jeremie said, touching her arm to pull her away as he dropped more payment onto the table for Lola's services.

When they were a distance away, Ginny asked, "Do you think she could see?"

This moment reminded Ginny of a long ago conversation with her bunkmates, wondering about magic.

"No. It is only entertainment. She didn't even want to look into the future and see that the kingdom will be fine. She wants to benefit from others fears. That makes me feel a little sick. Let's go sit and have a drink."

Unfortunately, his reply had reminded her a little too much of Lydia.

He led her, returning to the long tables they had eaten at earlier.

Jeremie played the gracious king. He would talk to three or four villagers, then Luke would discourage others for a few minutes, thus allowing Jeremie to listen to music or play a game or drink a beer in peace. Then he would be available to talk to a few more subjects again. Unlike a usual day, no one was angry at him for the state of affairs of the kingdom. People blamed his father for the curse, which trickled down to Jeremie himself. He had been appointed by an anonymous witch to be their salvation, a promise that remained unfulfilled. But everyone was happy tonight. They were all in good spirits, literally. The beer kept flowing. Ginny had never tasted it before, and it was nasty. She couldn't bring herself to finish her mug until Jeremie started his third. She felt left out and wanted to be as jolly as everyone else. Finishing her one mug made her equally as drunk as Jeremie. At that point, she did not care what it tasted like.

Ginny's giant head, which often hurt her neck to hold it up, felt even heavier as it bobbed from side to side. Everything made her giggle. Candles and torches had been lit to outline a stage and dance floor in the village square. The flames were beautiful, especially slightly blurry as they were to her inebriated eyes.

The strolling musicians retired from their duties. A band took the stage and started to play. They were loud and raucous.

Everyone began to clap. Some brave souls ran out to the dance floor. Ginny chuckled at them.

"C'mon, dance with me!" Jeremie yelled to her above the ruckus. "I haven't gotten to dance in such a long time." He grabbed her hand and tried to drag her with him, but she sat firm on her wooden bench.

"No way! I can't dance!" she screamed at him, starting to laugh hysterically at his invitation. She never laughed. It felt weird. She could feel her double chins jiggle.

"Sure you can! It's easy, see?" With that, Jeremie stood at the edge of the dance floor directly in front of Ginny and began to jump up and down and flail his arms. The crowd went wild with hoots and hollers at the celebrity in their midst. Once she could find her breath again, she screamed, "You look ridiculous!"

"So, you can't look any sillier. Join me." He offered his hand to her.

"But I don't know how to dance," she whined.

"It's easy. Let me show you." And with that, she let herself be towed out onto the dance floor by Jeremie. She giggled at how ridiculous all this had become; leaving the orphanage, working with the king, being his friend, dancing with him. She was positive she would not have agreed to this had it not been for the beer.

Ginny hopped once, then twice. Then she just stood still and tried to watch the other dancers around her, to see what moves they were doing. What position were their arms in? Their legs? But they were all moving too fast, spinning around her.

"Here, please let me help you," Jeremie said, smiling at her. His cheeks were rosy from the alcohol. His smile was so wide she was afraid it would swallow her up. But she thought that may be the perfect way to die.

Jeremie held her right hand in his left. He moved her left hand to his shoulder. Then he placed his free hand onto her hip. She snorted at him.

"What? What's wrong?"

"That tickles."

He rolled his eyes the color of cocoa at her, and then tried to catch the beat of the music. Luckily, the band changed songs to something that was still up-tempo, but not as frantic as their first song had been. It allowed Jeremie to teach her how to move her feet.

It was difficult for her. The alcohol made her sluggish and her feet were twice as wide as his. But he was patient with her. He seemed to enjoy teaching her.

The next song was a slow, sad one. Jeremie pulled her close enough that she could lay her head against his chest. His clothes smelled of fresh air and sweat. She looked up at his face. His eyes were closed as they danced to the music. His hair hung down in sweaty clumps across his forehead. It had been allowed to grow too long. Black stubble dotted his chin, making him look older than his nineteen years. There were specks of mud on his clothes from riding all day, and tiny tears at the seams. Where his hand held hers, she could tell that he had dirt under his fingernails.

"What?" he asked, when he caught her studying him.

"You are a disgrace to the title of king, you know that?" she barked at him.

"Aw fuck, who cares. Our kingdom might end tomorrow anyhow." A cloud of sadness passed across his eyes. He blinked and it was gone. But she had seen it. She now knew he had his doubts that all of this could be saved. His earlier comment about the kingdom being fine had been a bluff. He was just keeping it to himself.

The music picked up again, and their dancing did accordingly. The footwork came easier to her. Jeremie would throw in a spin every now and then. Once he made her spin him. People around them laughed. They didn't laugh at them, but with them. Ginny hadn't known there was a difference between the two. In this environment, it was easy to forget who they were and what others thought of them. Ginny wanted Jeremie to spin her around, and to be this happy forever. The flames flickered all around her in bright streaks as he spun her. Friendly faces laughed and talked around her. The candles began to burn out, one by one, then two by two.

Ginny's legs ached, but it was a good kind of pain, much like the one slowly burning in her heart. Considering the king's traveling party had all been tired when they arrived, they were all dead on their feet after partaking in the festivities. Ginny had even seen stoic Luke have a few beers and smile tonight. Ginny was parched, drinking a whole second beer. But this one made her drowsy.

She and Jeremie leaned against each other for support as they made their way to the town inn. All the rooms had been full, but of course one had been made available for the king. There were three tiny beds in the room, one each for Jeremie, Ginny, and Luke. They chuckled at how small they were, except for Luke who eyed the beds suspiciously. He was six inches taller than both of them. Jeremie took the bed nearest the door, Ginny took the bed in the center, and Luke took the one nearest the window. A guard was posted outside the door. Jeremie and Ginny giggled until their laughs turned into snores.

## BURN

I had given up
on my appearance
on myself
on giggles and tingles
on lust.

I look in the mirror
and tell myself
"You are so ugly
You are so old
No one is attracted to you."

Then YOU walked into my life.
YOU made me remember
what it was like to
have an obsession
a crush
that was not trapped
inside a book.

YOU always pass by
with a very stern look
on YOUr face.
But I found that I could bring out
YOUr smile.

And what a smile it is!
It raises YOUr black eyebrows
And puts a twinkle in YOUr
BROWN EYES.

Do YOU realize that
when I lay eyes on YOU
my heart actually picks up speed?

Do YOU realize that just
seeing YOU for 10 seconds makes
my day?
my week?

I would flirt with YOU
if I knew how.
Knowing I will see
YOU
makes me want to
dress up
wear jewelry
do my hair.

I want to
be pretty
for YOU
although I know I shouldn't.
But I cannot help
what ignites my
dormant heart
gives me back
giggles
tingles
lust
HEAT.

And YOU make me burn brighter than EVER before.

The next morning, Ginny and Jeremie had terrible headaches. Luke knew what root they should chew to alleviate their pain, and it worked. Luke was much more than the lead guard. He showed it with his intelligence and loyalty every day.

They proceeded to set up a kissing booth at the faire that day for the king, instead of going door-to-door as they generally did. They all agreed it was the quickest way to make their way through all the women in town. It drove Ginny nuts because she was the one sitting behind the table with the ledgers trying to figure out who lived together in which household. It made it difficult that many of the villagers could not remember the numbers recently hung on their house. Still others could not read them. Most could not remember the new names given to the roads.

That night they only had one beer each. They mapped out where they would head the next day, and went to bed. Ginny couldn't help but feel sad. She knew she would never get the chance to feel again like she had last night. She had felt accepted, loved. She had felt like a queen.

On a warm, cloudless night, Jeremie and Ginny sat out on a blanket under the stars. It was late July. Enjoying time outside like this at night was commonplace when they were young. Lately, there was often an unexplained chill in the air. But this was a last little gift before the end folded in around them.

"Do you remember when I found you in the barn?" she asked.

"How could I forget," he said with levity.

"Did you hide like that often?"

"As often as I could manage. I realize I was born into an incredibly blessed life. But that doesn't mean I was always happy to throw myself into it. Everyone needs their quiet moments."

Ginny nodded her head. "That is how I felt about farm work."

"You felt like work was an escape? I'm not sure I understand."

"Work is not always a bad thing, Your Highness," she said, poking fun at him.

"Of course I snuck off a lot. How do you think I always know where to find you in the castle?"

"Ah, it all makes sense. But I never find you hiding now."

"I think when I came of age, I replaced hiding by myself with being in the company of girls."

"Women. And, I have noticed that. Doesn't seem to happen as often anymore. Are you running out of warm bodies?"

"Nah. Just trying to cut back."

They were quiet for a while. Ginny thought of how the acceptance of her by Jeremie, and later Luke, is a gift she would cherish forever. It saved her soul from the abyss.

"Can you actually believe there was a time when people cared about money? They cared about coins to save and hoard. The coins had a value separate from the goods they could be used to purchase," Jeremie informed her, as they sat in the meadow, gazing up at the stars.

"I know that is how things used to be. But it was so long ago," Ginny replied.

"That is because the plague made food such a commodity that purchasing it with money eventually got to be silly. Food is valued among all else. The only thing as valuable to trade for it is other food, or medicine. People used to fight over money. They used to die for it. Hell, my father removed citizens from their farms for delinquent taxes. I think he actually enjoyed it. But the plague makes that all silly. We will all die any day now. We have to treasure each day that remains in our lives. I mean, people used to stay up at night to count their money. It is unbelievable. I haven't even collected taxes since my father died. And for the last decade, he was accepting food and livestock."

"I think I prefer to count the stars," Ginny said, laying her head down on the blanket, staring straight up at the heavens.

"Ya, me too," Jeremie said, assuming an identical position.

He reached out and took her hand. Ginny liked to think that her hand was the only thing holding him to the earth, preventing him from floating up toward the almost full moon. A ring of smoke from the party's nearby campfire encircled it and glowed silver, a halo in the sky. They both gripped as tightly as they could to the last bit of hope that still resided in their hearts.

Ginny continued traveling with Prince Jeremie in search of *the one*. Having no success, her mood became darker, just as Jeremie's did. It felt as though his failure was now her own. Her heart ached for him. Previously when he was around, her heart beat faster and felt like it was glowing. Now it felt dark and decayed, tired. If Ginny thought too hard about all of it, she had to clutch her chest to keep her heart from bursting.

He never smiled anymore. That had been what Ginny had loved about him most. First the curse had killed the plants, then the animals, then the very old and the very young. Now it seemed as if it was killing him as well.

s life in the kingdom began to just fall away, so to did many of the pretenses of royal life. When traveling, they now slept in the same quarters, although in different beds, talking strategy until they fell asleep.

One night Ginny was awakened by Jeremie shouting. She sat up in bed and lit a candle. Luke quickly swung the door open, for he had been in the next room.

"Just a dream, I think," Ginny whispered to Luke as he scanned the room for a threat.

"A nightmare, I'd say," he declared, then backed out, returning whence he came.

"No, no. It can't be. I must stop it. There has to be a way. Where *is* she?"

Ginny walked to his bedside. She tried to think of a way to comfort him. Then his words turned to sobs. She wanted to be motherly, but resisted the urge to touch or pat him. Commoners did not go around touching kings while they slept. It just wasn't done. Plus, she really had no experience calming anyone. Even in her last days, Miss Peters had still been a reassuring presence to Ginny. With her last breath, she had still been a teacher and a guardian, giving Ginny lessons she would need to carry on in the world without her. Miss Peters never could have imagined what life would have in store for Ginny after her demise. The woman who once hid her from the king was probably rolling over in her grave that Ginny had dug at the fact that she now traveled the kingdom with one. Miss Peters had always taken care of Ginny, taught her to be a contributing citizen. She thought Ginny could master household and farm chores, but never expected that she could be a leader among royalty.

Jeremie's consciousness moved into a half-awake state. She sat down beside him on the bed. He startled Ginny by wrapping his arms around her, burying his head in her lap and continued to cry. Sobs emptied from deep inside him. More naturally than she ever could have imagined, she enfolded her arms around him. She always forgot how warm other people were until she touched them. Her stubby fingers always had poor circulation.

"Shhh. We will figure this out. It's not your fault," Ginny consoled him softly. She did not say "Everything will be OK." They all knew time was running out for that to be an option. Jeremie's fragileness scared her. He was the king. He wore a crown and stood on a balcony of a great stone castle while flags with his family crest flew around him. He was supposed to be infallible.

It was obvious; the curse was actually hurting Jeremie more than it ever had his father. She swore right then and there that she would kill that witch, if she ever found her. It had turned a smart, promising young man into a broke pile of young boy, seeking comfort from a troll.

Ginny could not hold back her own tears. She folded herself over Jeremie, burying her face into his black hair. It quickly became wet with her tears, as did her skirt with his. They held each other tightly, allowing no thoughts or worries or curses to invade their world, made up of only the bed they sat on at this moment in the night. They sat like that for a long time until the sun began to rise over the mountains. When his faculties returned, Jeremie thanked her for understanding. Side by side, they prepared a breakfast of biscuits and oatmeal. They would not speak of their night in front of the guards. There were already rumblings among them that the end was near. The same gray whispers were spreading through the villages as well. No reason to give them more fuel for the fire. Jeremie and Ginny stoically rode their horses. They did not attempt to hide their exhaustion.

As much as Ginny didn't like how considerably the end-of-time nightmare had upset Jeremie, she could admit, with a guilty conscience, that she had enjoyed being the only one he could seek comfort from. She had felt as though she were trying to hold him together as she soothed him.

Ginny tried to ignore her urges, knowing the end of the kingdom was near and she would be free of this ache in her heart soon. But she could not help that she still wanted Jeremie. Not because he was the king, as all the others did, but because he had grown to be her best friend. Sure, it had blossomed on this excursion, but the building blocks had really been laid all those years ago, in the marketplace and at the orphanage. He wasn't perfect, but she could chalk a lot of that up to his upbringing. He had been given everything he wanted his whole life, leaving him spoiled and naïve at how to obtain the one thing that would save all the people.

*Where is the most beautiful girl?*

Sometimes Ginny was awakened at night by Jeremie, chanting the refrain over and over as he slept. Every morning he would be more lost and deflated than the night before. She wished her holding him again would make it all well.

If he held her, it would be even better. It wasn't like she didn't have her own doubts about the viability of the kingdom.

When they walked through the last settlement, Jeremie's eyes searched eagerly from face to face, desperately searching for the most beautiful girl that could save the land. Villagers ran up to the king sobbing, hanging on him, pleading for him to stop the famine, to stop the death. Luke would pry them off, but the king was visibly disturbed. He seemed on the brink of tears himself. Ginny's closeness seemed to be the only thing holding him together.

As they prepared to travel back to the castle, with no success, two of the guardsmen themselves fell ill. They had been in the prime of their lives and in peak physical condition. They could not hold on to their lives for the week it took to make it back to the castle.

There was a moving ceremony to commemorate their service at their interment. It was outside, although it was late August and the weather was filled with chill. Jeremie wanted Ginny to stand with the other guardsman. He said she had earned it. She declined, explaining to him that those who had not made the journey would not understand why she was being given such an honor. She didn't want to cause a commotion that would distract from solemn purpose of the event.

After the ceremony, Ginny found a hidden spot, behind one of the corners of the castle, to be alone with her thoughts. She wrapped her arms around her body, trying to squeeze out the cold. She had her heavy coat on, but it wasn't helping on this occasion. The cold felt as though it was leaking out of Ginny herself. She heard voices approaching and shrunk back further, out of sight.

"I never thought I would see the day when we would be burying Carlos and Rafael," a voice said, disgusted. Ginny could not place it.

"Erik, it is better they go now, so that we can honor them," Jeremie replied.

Ginny remembered Erik as a young guard who had not made the trip.

"There will be no one left to bury or remember us when the end comes to the rest of us," he continued.

"So it is hopeless then, Your Majesty? Have you given up on finding the one who shall break the curse?" Erik implored.

"Aye. I am convinced that no such being exists."

"If only you had taken me with you on the search instead of that ugly troll, then you would have found success."

Ginny winced at Erik's words. "Troll" already implied unattractiveness. Why did he have to call her out as ugly too yet? Apparently he was still bitter that Ginny had gone on the eight month mission instead of him. She wondered how many others in the castle felt the same way. If only they had known the truth: the saddle sores from riding all day, the unrelenting cold, the increasing hopelessness that had eventually overtaken them, brought them to this place of despair Jeremie now toiled in daily. She remained quiet as she waited for Jeremie to defend her.

"Perhaps taking her was a bad decision. It had its merits at the time," Jeremie reasoned.

"What the f—" escaped out of Ginny's mouth before she clamped her hands over it. The brisk wind hid her comment from their nearby ears. What was that? The greatest adventure of her whole life, one bringing self-worth and self-esteem into her existence, was a mistake? She held herself tighter, not from the cold this time, but from the men's uncensored words.

"You wasted lots of valuable time with all that organizing crap," Erik spat.

"The records did take a long time. But I don't feel as though it was a total waste. " Jeremie sounded tired, defeated.

"Of course it was a waste! What are those documents good for now? It will be just a list of names of a bunch of dead people. "

"And what would you have done?" he asked, seeming genuinely interested.

"The high priests wouldn't approve, but I think I have the expertise of Mother Nature on my side."

"What are you getting at, kiddo?"

"The wild! The male lion sleeps with as much female tail as possible. If you cannot *find* the most beautiful girl, why not *make* one!" Erik declared excitedly.

Ginny's stomach churned. She fell to her knees and dry-heaved. Skipping breakfast and lunch today had turned out to be a good call. She hated that his words could make her physically ill. Erik was a creep and she never wanted him to have any effect on her. Ever.

"So, you are saying I should knock up every woman in the kingdom?"

'Why were they still even discussing this?' Ginny wondered.

"Well, only the hot ones. And you have anatomy in your favor. You only need one schlong to impregnate many, many woman. They could all gestate at the same time. And think of the fun you would have! There is still time to implement it, if you started right away."

"I had given up, already used our last-ditch effort. But there are a lot of lives at stake. If there is another option… And don't all father's think that their daughter is the most beautiful girl in the world?" he mused.

Ginny lay in the grass, covering her ears, silently begging them to stop talking about this. Why was Jeremie entertaining such an idea? And why couldn't they all just die already? Their death sentence had been written two decades ago.

"See? But you would have to leave your bow-wow BFF at home. She would probably scare the fertility right out of the other chicks. My God, her face looks like my horse's ass. Probably that is how Carlos and Rafael died, having to look at that moly face every day killed them. Makes me glad I wasn't part of that caravan."

Ginny could still hear them, but not for long. She got up and ran in the opposite direction of where they were still talking. She knew this was the long way around to reenter the castle, but she didn't care. She wanted the safety of her chambers, and to hide in her room and never come out to face anyone ever again, until the end of time.

The task force continued to have daily meetings, mostly about the status of the environment, lives lost, and the dwindling supplies of food and fresh water. It was not pleasant and it wasn't necessarily mandatory, so Ginny stopped going. She couldn't get over the things that had been said about her in Jeremie's presence, which he had not defended. She contemplated leaving the castle altogether, but she knew she had nowhere else to go. At least all this was coming to an end soon, this painful existence where her heart felt more broken with every human interaction. Fuck them all. She wouldn't go down for meals either. She could have the handmaiden bring up her food. There was not much more than biscuits and vegetable stew left to consume, the vegetables from jars canned and stored from past, more bountiful harvests.

On the third day of this new solitary routine, she heard a knock at her door. It wasn't time for a handmaiden to be there. She stayed where she was, seated on her bed with a book. If she didn't move, maybe they wouldn't know she was there and would go away. Next to her were a stack of the next books she would read, and a stack she already had finished. Fewer trips to the library meant less chance of running into someone she didn't want to see in the halls, namely, the owner of this whole damn pile of rock.

There was another knock, more forcefully this time. It was definitely a man. Could it possibly be Jeremie, come to apologize for the misunderstanding? She stared at the door, weighing her options. Even if that was the case, she wasn't done being upset with him yet.

"Ginny. I know you are in there. Open up" came the familiar voice. Not Jeremie, he always used her full name. It was Luke. He had always been kind to her, even sharing a tent to protect her when no one else would. The chances of him coming to spread salt into her wounds were slim, especially since the only one who still used the limited supply of salt was the king.

Ginny walked over and swung open the door, taking a step back for Luke to enter. His blond, wavy hair now almost reached his shoulders.

"I expected to be out there all day knocking," he said.

"I take it this isn't a social call, then?"

He ran his hand through his hair, and then placed it on the handle of his sword. She wondered why he even still wore it. No one was invading. Did he think he would be able to slay the blackness when it came for them?

"Why haven't you left your chamber in days?" Luke was never one to beat around the bush.

"How did you even notice?"

"How could I not? The task force has all but disbanded entirely, there is no one to tell sad stories that make us all feel better about our over-privileged childhoods, and most of all, my best friend is pouting and being way too clingy."

"Your best friend?"

"Don't play dumb with me. You are better than that."

"Why would he be moping?" Neither of them mentioned Jeremie by name.

"Maybe you aren't playing."

"Hey! Are you calling me dumb?" Ginny spat.

"If you can't see that he cares for you, then the word fits."

"You might as well call me dumb. Jeremie already called me ugly."

"I find that rather hard to believe."

"He may as well have," Ginny said, her voice wavering.

"So technically he didn't?"

"He was talking to Erik. Jeremie," her voice cracked, "didn't defend me."

Luke busted out laughing. That was the last straw. She had felt safe in his presence. But now it was clear that he was just as big a threat to her self-esteem as the rest of the royal lot.

"Go! Get the hell out!" Ginny threw open the door and stomped her foot. Luke pushed the door closed again, his uproar dissolving into chuckles.

"Ginny, Erik is a dumbass. If Jeremie didn't stand up for you, he didn't feel like getting into it with Erik right then. "

"It was Carlos and Rafael's funeral…"

"See? You know Erik is a hothead. Jeremie probably was just humoring him to keep the peace."

"So, what about Plan B?"

"What Plan B?" Luke asked, dumbfounded.

"Nevermind," Ginny dismissed his question, embarrassed.

"So, will you come downstairs for dinner tonight? It would mean a lot to the king."

Oh, now he was back to being a person of authority again.

"If it would mean so much to him, why isn't he here pleading his case? Did he send you to do his dirty work?" she said, her words sounding as snotty as she meant for them to be.

"No. He didn't have to."

"Oh, it is just in your job description then."

"Not as his knight, but as his friend."

"I don't think I can make it."

"I'm Jeremie's best friend. Well, his best male friend. It is obvious to me that he cares for you. And he doesn't think that you are ugly." His bright blue eyes met hers. It seemed he believed the words he spoke.

"I don't believe you. Jeremie has never told me any such thing," she said, calling his bluff.

"True. But he has demonstrated it. In his actions, in his loyalty to you, you will find the truth you so desperately seek."

"Has he really said that?"

"What?"

"That I'm not ugly. Or are you just saying that to make me feel better."

"I swear," he answered, raising his right hand as if taking an oath to her. "Others have asked him, in my presence, why he would associate with you, how he could stand to. He has told me that he doesn't see what all the fuss is about. You have such a kind and helpful heart. He counts you as one of his dearest and most trusted friends," he paused. "We all know... Well, now is not the best time to let opportunities pass you by," he finished, alluding to the end of their days.

"Thank you." Ginny squeaked the words out past the lump in her throat.

"So you will?"

"Yes. That is, if you will come and escort me."

"No problem," he smiled, his eyes twinkling.

At the appointed dinner hour, Luke knocked on her door. Ginny couldn't help it; she was excited to be leaving her room. She had even put on her nicest dress. She slid the only piece of jewelry that she owned over her head, the blue stone hanging from her neck. Ginny still did not understand why the mystery woman at the faire had given it to her. Maybe the woman had seen something that Ginny herself had not. Maybe Jeremie had always been her friend, and she wouldn't let herself accept that, never thought she deserved such happiness. Ginny had come to believe that her insides were screwed up, that she was as weird on the inside as the outside. The girls at the orphanage had made her believe that. But she actually felt better tonight, whole, as she walked into the dining hall to a table of familiar faces, headed by the king himself. She was one of Jeremie's best friends. That warmed her heart.

Jeremie's face lit up at her entrance. It warmed more than her heart. She could never stop herself from wanting more of him. What if she had been normal inside all along? It was a pain she would have to bear. She couldn't decide if being lonely and ugly was worse, or if being close to someone you loved but couldn't have in that fulfilling, whole way was. Right now it felt like the latter.

"I'm glad you could join us tonight. I trust you are feeling better," he said jovially, winking at her. The ache within her would not subside.

"Yes. Thank you."

Luke pulled out a chair from the table, allowing her to take a seat. He took his own place across from her. They sat on either side of Jeremie. Ginny had replaced the ladies who used to giggle and coddle the king nightly. She felt some satisfaction at this observation.

She looked down the table and noticed an empty seat. It belonged to Cassian. Ginny looked from the empty chair to Luke, asking him a silent question. He gave a small nod of his head in reply, and then looked down to concentrate on his food.

So that was how it was now. The plague had moved on from children and the elderly into those in the prime of their lives. How much longer did any of them have left? First Carlos and Rafael, now Cassian.

Jeremie, seeming to miss the exchange, leaned over to Ginny.

"You are looking nice tonight, Guinevere," he whispered huskily to her.

"Thank you," she managed to reply. She had gotten dressed up for him, but never expected him to notice, let alone compliment her.

It momentarily lifted her spirts again to where they had been after her conversation with Luke.

G inny had gone down to the library to choose a new book. The more the world deteriorated outside her window, the more she found herself retreating into fiction to escape from it. Tonight she had sat down to browse through a new one she had not yet read. A few hours later, she came to realized she was curled up in a ball in a padded chair in front of the fire, eighty pages into the story. She would have been content to spend the entire night there alone. That is, until Jeremie entered the room.

His face said everything that the words that would not escape through his lips didn't. Something had upset him. Ginny stood and approached him. She reached out to take his hand, and that is when she realized he was holding a book. It was the book of Inniskellin history she had given him as a gift, almost a year ago.

"Guinevere," he began, but forgot to finish. She led him over to the couch to sit, taking a place beside him.

"Is it the book? I never meant for it to upset you." She began to rub his back, hoping she could coax the words out of him. It eventually yielded the result she was hoping for.

"It, it's bad."

"What is?"

"I always knew… but I didn't."

"You aren't making sense." She watched as he took a deep breath before continuing.

"I always knew that my father was kind of a jerk, but, now I know—"

"What do you know?"

"It was my father. We are cursed because of him."

"What are you taking about?"

"The big question. I always wondered why the witch chose our kingdom to curse. She didn't choose. My father's actions drove her to it."

"What are you talking about?"

"Here, read this." He handed the book to her. She opened it up to where his thumb had kept the page.

*Something strange happened today. I was one of those people who always believed that magic was just a slight of hand, someone's trick of the eye. But that witch today seemed awfully real. Wait, this is to be an official record.*

*King Talbot attended the faire at Olicken today. He spent hours there, with several ladies on his arm. There was a commotion when he turned down a dance request from an old woman. I will never forget her face: beady eyes, large nose, rotten teeth.*

*How do I write what happened next?*

*How do I not write what happened before?*

*I would protect Tal with my life, if it came to that. I respect his position. He is my friend. He knows how to have a good time.*

*But, God damn, Tal is an asshole.*

*He could have just politely told her his dance card was full, that he had no time due to official business.*

*But no, he had to go and call her ugly, call her retarded, insult her vagina, then call her a witch. If the king should ever happen to have a son, as the curse mentions, he should never know everything that was said on this day to bring about this chain of events. He would hang me if he knew I thought this, but I think he deserved to be cursed for what he said. Someone should have done it sooner. If only I thought that it would set him straight.*

*What kills me is it seemed to not have any effect on him whatsoever. If this comes to pass, it will spell certain doom for all of us one day. I have a newborn son. I don't want him to grow up in an age of suffering.*

*It went unspoken that all the members of the royal party would minimize what happened today. But I need to put it somewhere. I will hide this book now. If you are lucky enough to find it, then you are one of the few who knows the truth.*

*And maybe you managed to survive the curse. Send the most beautiful girl my regards. I sure would love to meet her. She must be quite a gal.*

"It's the final entry," Jeremie stated, even as her fingers greedily flipped ahead for more information, only making contact with a series of blank pages. He took it back from her. "This was my father's fault. All the lives lost, including his wife's and his own. They could have all been prevented if he had just had some human decency. If anything, my father is the *only* one who deserved to die."

He was crying now. Ginny tried to hug him, but he pushed her away and stood. He began to pace back and forth in front of the fire.

"I hate him. I *hate* him."

"He was a shitty king."

"Yes." Jeremie turned to glare at her as the light from the fire's flames danced on his chiseled features, made more piercing by his anger.

"But he is the only father you ever had. And you have spoken fondly of him. You even named a road after him."

"Ya, I'm gonna have to fix that. My father not only didn't tell me, he downright lied to me. He always said he had no idea why she cast the curse, that she was just wicked."

"Maybe he didn't know."

"What? You read the entry."

"Yes. And maybe King Talbot didn't see anything wrong with what he said. The witch tried to get the point across, but it never worked. He died still thinking he had every right to say such things to her."

"You are not helping."

"I'm sorry," Ginny said softly, and then she hugged him, attempting to calm him down.

# UNTITLED

You just always seem to catch me
At my most genuine moments
Those times when I'm sparkling
And not even realizing it

Some people must go about their lives, the days stretching out into a never-ending expanse ahead of them. Ginny had always accepted that her days were numbered. It had never caused her great anxiety. She had spent so much time just trying to get through one day after another. But now that the end was near, well, her body felt empty and cold and useless. Preparing for the grave already, she supposed.

At first, there were only a few hours of daylight every day—the rest was the darkness of the total absence of light, even the stars no longer appeared. Then perpetual clouds blocked any of the sun's rays from reaching them. They could see in those few hours outside without the aid of torches, but it was still too dim in the castle to move about unaided. It was as if a great blanket had been made to cover the kingdom. It made them all sad, on edge, smothered by their own depression. They no longer yearned for the sunny days of just months before. Now they all prayed that death would take them swiftly—and soon. It was a depression sickness that was suffocating them, from the inside out.

Then the storms came. Big black clouds billowing with lightning and thunder filled the sky and the void left by the lack of the sounds of birds and insects. The rain drops were as big as Ginny's hands. The remaining royal party remained inside. Other surviving villagers came to stay in the lower floors of the castle. Rations were running low. Ginny had taken to helping prepare food. With a considerable amount of the maids having passed on, there was a lack of useful hands. It helped to fill up the long emptiness of the dark days. She had overcome so much adversity in her upbringing, to rise in the ranks and dabble with the most decorated knights, only to find herself back in the kitchen. She had abandoned the library and its books. Her thirst for knowledge had dried up.

Jeremie kept to his chamber now. He was well enough physically to leave it, but he had no motivation to. Ginny took him his meals. Finding out the truth about the curse had been too much for him. He never recovered after that to the jovial state he had once perpetually lived in.

He was different tonight. She sensed it in the air as soon as she entered the room. Jeremie was standing by the small window, the draperies pulled back. The storm churned like a vicious mythological beast. Sometimes the thunder rolled on for minutes at a time. The wind was whipping the rain into the room, onto Jeremie. He turned as she entered and she could see that his hair and the front of his clothes were soaked.

"Jeremie, what are you thinking? Step away from there now," she nagged him as if she were his mother and he her child. She sat the dinner tray on a nearby table and moved across the room to where he stood. She tried to pull him back from the window and close the draperies, but he resisted.

"It won't be long now," he said, as if in a trance. He pointed into the distance. He continued, "See the bottom of the mountains, where they meet what used to be the green hills of our youth?"

The clouds had covered the mountains for days. And the hills had not been green for several years.

"Yes. Why does it look hazy?"

"That is the curse. It is turning them into nothing."

"What?" Ginny replied, shocked. She guessed no amount of inevitability could fully prepare her.

"The mountains have been gone for a few days. The curse is now ripping the hills up into tiny bits, spinning them around in a million mini-cyclones, and then *poof*—they are gone."

"Ugh. Straight for us."

"The castle is the last on the hit list. Like the witch wanted me to witness the destruction until the end."

"That is ridiculous. She never even met you. It was your father who should have had to break the spell."

"But it wasn't. It was foretold to be me, and I have failed."

"It may have always been impossible to stop it. Come, let's get you out of these wet clothes," she urged.

This time he let her pull him back from the sill and close the drapes. She ran her hand over his wet hair, trying to wring some water out of it. His hair was so black she expected the liquid coming out of it to be as dark as crude oil. Her fat fingers fumbled with the bejeweled buttons on his velvet overcoat. She felt Jeremie gazing down at her, but she ignored him. Finally reaching the bottom, she pushed the coat up to his shoulders, and then pulled it off his arms, trying not to linger on the tight muscles there. Her hand touched his chest, his undershirt damp against her outstretched palm.

"Oh dear. This is wet too," she fretted.

Jeremie placed both his hands over hers on his chest, moving them slightly to cover his heart. It beat strong in his chest.

"Lay with me."

"What?" she squealed without thinking.

"Be with me now. You are so special to me, always have been. Please share these last moments of time with me. Please?"

He was begging her. And he didn't even need to be. She had already been weakened by his presence when she had entered into his chamber. He was vulnerable, lost. He was standing there, his hair damp. Then she was undressing him. She had done it out of a sense of nurturing and duty. But it was more the act of a wife than a mother. Her thoughts were not pure as she stood this close to him.

"I have never understood what other people see when they look at you. I have never seen a monster."

He said the perfect words she had always wanted to hear. And they meant the most coming from him. She knew what she was. A horrible, ugly, little gross troll gurl. She knew this in her heart. It hurt as she reminded herself. And Jeremie's dark, pleading eyes were breaking it as well. If he had lost his mind and wanted to be with her for the night, why not?

Ginny had common sense. She knew how society looked at females who did this sort of thing before they had a husband. But she was a troll. He was a hot king. The world was ending outside the castle window. She might never get this chance again.

"I am not going to kiss you," he explained. "Kisses for me have always had an expectation that went unfulfilled. They always left me with disappointment."

She slowly nodded her head in agreement. If he was willing to take what she offered, and give himself to her, it didn't seem important, that one small detail.

As her mind was already set on removing his shirt, she did. She let her hands touch the muscular chest she had only caught glimpses of before as he dressed when they had shared quarters on the road. It was hard, like a stone, but hot. He wrapped his arms around her, pulling her close. He squeezed her tightly, nuzzling the side of her neck below her ear.

"Guinevere," he sighed. "Be my touchstone, as you have so many times before. I would never have made it this far without you."

"No, no. I—"

"Shhh," he cooed into her ear. "You know it is true. And I hope I was a comforting force for you as well. "

"Always," she breathed. She had faith now that he would be in this moment with only her, not thinking of any of his many past conquests that she had mistakenly thought he found more appealing than herself. She let her lips touch his neck. She sucked at his skin. The taste of salt and rain danced on her tongue.

His left hand pushed into the small of her back, the right squeezed her buttocks lightly, as if gauging how far she wanted to go. But she was all in, as she hoped he soon would be. Her body responded quickly to his touch, as if it already knew what was coming, which was impossible. She had never been touched by a man other than receiving assistance mounting and dismounting a horse.

Well, there were Jeremie's squeezes and hand-holds of friendship. Of course there was the time she had danced with Jeremie at the faire. He pushed her to arm's length now, and she smiled up at him, remembering that moment, not so long ago. She had been full of hope for finding the chosen girl, and a silly belief in a future with the king. Those dreams had fallen to the wind. What they had now would be short and sweet.

They began to untie and loosen the drawstrings on the front of her dress at the same time. She probably could have done it faster by herself, but the little jolts of electricity that ran through her fingers every time they touched his were worth the delay. When it was loosened, he drew her arms up straight, and then pulled the dress off over her head. The dying fire and a few torches provided the only flickering light. She worried that he wouldn't like what he saw. The dress's corset always gave her gelatinous body some sort of shape. Standing before him in only her white slip, she didn't know how much he would notice.

He crushed her against him in a passionate embrace. Something hard pressed against her lower abdomen. She realized it was his erect member. He wasn't going through the motions for her benefit. He was actually attracted to her. She was thrilled, wrapping her hands around the back of his neck, preparing to pull him into a kiss. Then she remembered his ground rules. Actually "rule," as there had only been the one. Instead, their heads hung there, in space and time, locking eyes. A goofy smile spread across his face, as if he had a funny joke to tell her. But, she was in on it too and returned it as best she could without showing her teeth.

She hated that she was still self-conscious with him, even in this current situation that had arisen. But her body didn't seem to bother him as he ran his hands up and down it, approving grunts escaping his lips. They moved to her breasts, lingering and caressing them. He did it cautiously, as if still giving her a chance to stop him. There was not a chance in hell of that happening. His hands were at her hips, pulling her closer to him. The heat from their bodies became one, forcing all the ugly cold in the room away from them. They stood there, her in her slip and bloomers, him in only his long john pants.

Jeremie bent down in front of her. Her breath caught in her throat. He slid his hands up her legs, underneath her gown. The thin muslin rode up his arms. When he reached the waist of her bloomers, he carefully undid the two modest buttons there. Her heart was hammering in her chest. He tugged them down until they were a puddle at her feet. He rose back up. She kept touching him, never getting enough, wanting to rip his pants off and take what she wanted.

She was closer to fulfilling her wish when he led her over to his bed. She sat down on the edge as he began to draw the curtains of the canopy closed around them. It made it easier to pretend the turmoil outside wasn't real. He put a knee on either side of her hips, and slowly laid her back. He ran his fingers through her straight hair, looking at her adoringly.

He pulled up her gown, and with a roll to one side, then the other, causing Ginny to giggle, he removed it. She was now nakid, but he was not. She decided to remedy this undesirable situation.

She reached up to his waist and undid the hooks and eyes there. A slight moan escaped his lips. She began to push down his pants, but he quickly backed up and stood, in order to remove them more quickly himself. He then came back, leaning over her, searching her eyes once again for the permission she had already granted him.

She wanted a better look at his manhood, but that would have to wait. He placed his mouth over one of her nipples and began to suck it. Charges went through her body making it twist in ways it never had before. He smiled at her devilishly. It fanned the flames burning deep inside her. He took her other nipple in his mouth. At the same time, he slid a hand between her legs. She didn't know what he was going to do or how it would feel. He pulled a finger across her heat. She could tell how slippery her body was for him. It felt strange and wonderful. He did it more, now strumming her bud like a stringed instrument. This time her body lifted off the bed, even pushing him up as well.

"Whoa," he said, startled.

"Sorry," she responded out of habit.

"No. Don't be sorry. Don't ever be sorry," he said to her softly, nuzzling her forehead. Even after he had removed his nose, she swore she could feel energy circling there.

His hand was still busy between her legs. This time, he slid a finger inside of her. Her body contracted around it, without consulting her first. But it felt great. She rode his hand for another minute, enjoying the mind-blowing sensation. Then she grabbed onto his wrist, stopping him.

"Did I hurt you?" he asked, concerned.

"No," she hesitated. She didn't know what words to use, so she fumbled to grab a hold of his cock. She squeezed it gently.

"Ah," he said with satisfaction, figuring out that she wanted to give him pleasure too. He put his hand over hers, guiding it up and down his shaft in the rhythm that he liked.

He was still leaning over her as she stroked him. She enjoyed watching his beautiful face. The stress of the last year had accelerated his aging. He no longer looked like a boy, but a man. His eyes were closed, his mouth falling open, then closing again with each stroke. He stopped her hand and leaned his head down toward hers. What she had been admiring only seconds ago was now an inch from her own face. She moved in and he flinched, thinking she was headed for his mouth. But the kiss she planted landed on his cheek, as had always been her intention.

"You sure? You want this?" he confirmed, his voice husky with need.

"Yes," she said, meeting his dark eyes and holding them with her own. Of the parade of willing women Jeremie had bedded down, Ginny was glad she was the one here at the end.

He moved then, and she could feel his phallic head pushing against her. There was lots of pressure at first, not as good as everything else had been. Ginny wondered if something was wrong. But when Jeremie mumbled "so tight," she assumed this was how it was supposed to be. The pressure finally subsided, and he lay still inside her, filling her, as he looked down and smiled at her. Then he began to move in and out, quickly. It hurt at first, but then her body stretched to accommodate him. She felt the tension burning in her abdomen again. Before it had been pure, flaming pleasure, but his time it was a slow burn. It was actually painful, trying to reach again the summit of release. They panted as their bodies moved together.

"Oh Guinevere," he moaned. She felt his body tense under her fingers, him trying to hold back.

"Just Ginny," she breathed.

"Never," he demanded, a fire behind his dark eyes now.

She cried out, cold pain coursing through her before pleasure burned through her muscles behind it. Jeremie's body slowed then. He removed himself, lying next to her.

They remained like that for quite a while, him gently stroking her skin as the storm continued to roar. They could make out the sound of trees hitting the stones, the limbs and trunks cracking before they turned to dust, disintegrating. Chunks of stone, the castle itself breaking apart could be heard falling against the walls, stone on stone clattering in twisted wind funnels. When Ginny shivered, Jeremie fetched her gown, allowing her to dress. He put his pants back on, but nothing else. Ginny was glad because she was not done ogling his chest yet.

"I can't believe it is all ending," he said slowly.

"You know, Miss Peters once said that I was born at the instant the curse spread across the land. I think that was just a story she told, though. She would have no way to know that."

"It is a shame that your entire life shall be bookended and darkened by this curse," Jeremie said, tears in his eyes. "If I could have stopped it for no one else, I shall have liked to have stopped it for you."

"It has been a good life. It has especially improved today, even with my impending demise. You know, I would have stopped it for you, if I could have."

"Then we are just a bunch of wishers and dreamers, then."

"I suppose so. I am sorry that you ascended the throne just to watch your whole kingdom disappear into rubble."

"I would give all my nobility back to save my people."

"And that makes you the most noble of all."

Jeremie chuckled sadly. "I love you," he told her.

"I have always loved you," Ginny replied.

He leaned down and kissed her lips. He had told her that he would not, but she was elated that he had changed his mind. A tender piece of his affection, just for her. Ginny felt tears about to fall, but they suddenly disappeared. She felt Jeremie's lips slightly suck between her own, and then it was as if they were blown away. Ginny opened her eyes, but everything was so bright. The bed curtains were being blown upwards. Jeremie had backed away from her up against the wall, holding his arm across his body to protect himself. His hair blew in the giant wind that had come from nowhere. When she had found her breath, Ginny asked him, "Is this the end?"

"No! I think it may be the cure!"

His frightened face turned into a wide smile. Ginny, still not sure what was happening, wanted to treasure that smile as her last image as she left this world. She had loved his smile since she had first seen it as a girl, when he had helped her up off the ground at the market. But instead she was moving further away from him. Up toward the ceiling, in fact. It all made no sense.

Suddenly, they were not alone.

A wiry old woman with a frightening face appeared grinning in the bedroom with them.

"You finally figured it out, sonny. Right at the end, mind you. I had you all pegged for goners," she croaked.

"It's her! It's the witch who cast the spell on my father!" Jeremie explained to Ginny in a shout. The light and the wind was still all too much, intense and overpowering all their senses.

"What happened to my feet?! Why am I floating?" Ginny asked worriedly. She looked at her body as she looked at Jeremie and the witch below. Ginny's clothes had turned into a long ivory dress, with ribbons flying and jewels reflecting the light. She could see that her feet below her looked slender, as if they belonged to someone else, but she found they moved with commands from her mind.

"Dear girl, I always pegged you as the smart one of this duo," the witch laughed, but did not answer her.

"You said it yourself, Guinevere. You were born at the exact instant of the curse! That is why you came out the way you did. You were always the most beautiful girl in the land! You were the key!"

"What are you talking about? I'm a troll!" Ginny began to cry in disbelief. They both seemed to be making fun of her. She thought Jeremie understood how much that hurt.

"It was *inner beauty* that was always the key. Your father never learned that lesson, but you have," the witch explained. "Can't believe you traveled the land day after day together and never realized she was the one."

"Wait, so I had to suffer all this time, looking the way I did, because of the curse?" The light coming off Ginny was suddenly even brighter.

Jeremie was quick to reach up and grab her slender hand, drawing her closer to him.

"We all suffered, Guinevere. But now, don't you see? The suffering is over." He pulled her to him and kissed her again, a long, slow kiss that once again brightened her glow.

"Let me show you how you will spend the rest of your days, dearie," the witch said. Then she waved her hand and a mirror appeared from thin air into her gnarled grasp. She held it up, allowing Ginny to view herself.

Blond hair floated in soft curls above her head, the same color as the yellow light that emanated from her body. Piercing, sky-blue eyes blazed out from her perfectly symmetrical, blemish-free face. In the center of her face was a cute, tiny nose. So small, she did not see it at first. The image in the mirror reminded her of a china doll she had seen in a shop in the village in the shadow of the castle. The confused, beautiful girl stared back at her. She could not comprehend that the image she looked at was her own.

Jeremie pulled her back down to the ground, and she stayed there, connected to the earth by the usual forces again.

"Will the glow go away?" Ginny asked, extending out her arm, gazing at it. She turned it to the left, then to the right, and back again.

"Yes it will. It will go away in about nine months, when you have your baby. The glow will be transferred to your child."

Ginny and Jeremie looked at each other, confused.

"Hey, that's no curse. You guys did that all on your own," the witch chortled.

"But it was so, intense," Ginny whispered only to Jeremie, but of course the witch heard as well.

"It is supposed to be like that, when done right. That delicious type of pain you felt, well, that was your inner beauty trying to escape."

"This is way weird. A witch telling us about the birds and the bees," Jeremie said, rubbing a hand across the back of his neck.

A whole regiment of knights appeared at the door, swords drawn on all three of them. It had taken this long for the guards to realize they were not actually about to meet their own impending doom. Not knowing what was happening, they then rushed to the king's side in order to protect him from the undetermined threat. Some were in full plate armor, some only in chain mail.

"Time for me to go," the witch chirped, and pulled her cape around her.

"*No!*" Ginny screamed, her light becoming so bright that everyone in the room but her covered their eyes.

The knights all moved in a step closer to the witch, although many had legs that shook inside their armor.

"You have kept this kingdom locked under your evil grip for twenty years. Innocent people have died for the sins of just one. You must now pay for all that suffering," Ginny's voice deepened and thundered. "I vowed if I ever saw you, I would kill you!" Ginny knew it was insane. How would she, just a girl, ever kill a powerful witch? But she remembered that night that Jeremie had broken down in her arms and her resolve to find a way was strengthened.

The witch's response surprised her.

"You, dearie, are *the only one who can*," the witch squawked out each word as if it hurt her.

Ginny could tell Jeremie was itching to step in. He wanted to finish this himself.

"Because she is the one I gave the magic to," the witch continued, looking straight into Ginny's now clear eyes. "The power to break the curse was inside of her. The power to kill me is inside as well."

"I should be the one to do it. It was my kingdom she cursed," Jeremie announced, turning to Ginny. But she was already glowing brighter and starting to hum.

"No. I finish this," Ginny snarled.

And she summoned the hatred she had accumulated through the last twenty years of her life: every time someone had laughed at her, every rude comment, every time someone had physically tortured her. Ginny was able to channel it and aim it at the witch. Everyone ducked and turned away from the yellow light. The only two still standing were Ginny and the witch. When it seemed there might be no more hatred left to drain from her hair and skin and bones, she found one more well to tap.

"*I am not a troll! And I never was!*" Ginny screeched it out allowing for no one to ever doubt it again. The witch burst into a copper-ca-billion pieces of ash and dust.

Ginny returned to a much more reasonable glow. She was now more of a candle than a million torches.

"Is it over?" she turned to Jeremie, her eyes wide. Her voice was hoarse.

"Ya, I guess so... I just hope she doesn't have a sister."

"Haha, you are a laugh riot."

Silence fell in the room. The knights quickly searched the room for further threats, and then filed out the door. Luke removed his helmet, shaking out his blond hair before taking his place outside the door with a second guard.

"Wow. Oh, wow. The search for the most beautiful girl is finally over. I will have free time. My life will not be focused on one central purpose, as it has always been. I could begin to rebuild the kingdom," Jeremie paced, rubbing his hand across the back of his neck. "Huh, I have no idea what the day-to-day matters of running a kingdom are. My father never taught me. And now he can't." Jeremie's voice was wistful, his thoughts faraway.

"Just to remind you, you are not the only one to get your life back. All the remaining subjects in the kingdom have been released from their death sentence. My outsides finally match my insides! Now people will make snap judgments based on my appearance in a whole new way. I could do anything. Except, apparently, your seed has taken root in my garden. So, you may want to think about making an honest woman out of me." Ginny looked at him hopefully.

She was pretty now, but that did not guarantee that the prince would want her. He had found her good enough to have a roll in the hay with when the world as they knew it was ending, but marriage was forever. Forever had recently been transformed into a very long time, when it had not been before. And with the curse lifted, well he could search for true love now.

"Oh, God. Of course! We shall have a big, lavish wedding! All the surrounding kingdoms will be invited! Hopefully, they will no longer be too scared to come."

Ginny didn't want to say it. She didn't want him to have doubts about her if he did not already. But she had to know.

"But, you can marry anyone now, you know. You only needed me to break the curse. And it has been done," Ginny squeaked it out. Tears spilled from her eyes.

In that second that he stared at her and said nothing, her heart broke. She had let herself fall in love with Jeremie. She supposed she had been in love with him since the first time she laid eyes on him, that day in the market, when they were both children. And those feelings had only intensified in the recent months when she had been fortunate enough to spend every day with him. She had shown him all this today, before the arrival of the witch. She had never had such intense pleasant feelings for anyone before in her life. Without him, she didn't think she wanted to go on living, beautiful or not. Her body shook and she felt faint. Jeremie's hands grabbed her arms to hold her up.

"Of course I want to marry you! Were those cloudy eyes of yours also blind? God, I am overjoyed that you are the one! I always pictured it being some insipid, spoiled girl from in the shadow of the castle that my father would force me to marry when she turned out to be the one. You, you are everything I would want in a wife. You are my friend, you support me, you challenge me. In another time, with another set of priorities, I would have married you years ago."

"Really?" Ginny smiled. She couldn't wipe the wetness from her eyes or nose, as he was still holding her vertical by her arms.

"Of course," he smiled at her. "I have always checked on you over the years, haven't I? And for good or bad, you were easy to pick out of a crowd in your previous form. I knew the decision would never be mine anyway, thus it never crossed my mind. Plus, even without your looks, it would have been hard to convince anyone to let a royal marry a rag-tag orphan."

"But you are still a king and I am still an orphan."

"But now no one can deny that we are magic together."

They smiled at each other and then shared a long kiss that did not have to be anything other than a kiss. But her heart still sped up and she forgot how to breathe.

"Luke," he called, and the head of the knights left his post and returned to the room.

"Yes, Your Majesty," he addressed him as he bent on one knee in front of the king.

"Arise, for it is I who shall do the bowing before my beautiful bride. I need thee to witness."

Luke stood, and nodded his head in acknowledgement. Jeremie dropped to one knee in front of her and took her hands in his.

"Please bear witness that on the day the curse was lifted, as it shall be known from this day forward, King Jeremie does ask for Miss Guinevere's hand in marriage. And as she has no family to answer for her, let the answer that comes from her lips be good and true. What sayest thou?"

"Yes." Ginny was shaking. Jeremie hugged her tightly, pushing all the pieces of her back into place. He turned to Luke once again.

"She shall be known in an official capacity as Guinevere, Queen Consort, and be considered sovereign until the wedding takes place, and ever after."

When Ginny looked at Luke's face, he smiled and winked at her. She realized that not only was she giving him a full, wide toothy smile, but she was also laughing, right out loud.

L ifting the curse did not bring back the dead. No one really expected it to. Those still alive had all been seeking shelter inside the castle. The storm had obliterated everything around it. The castle survived, but would need extensive repairs. It had been the last island of life in Inniskellin. It was discovered by royal search party that the mountains and hills and trees were restored to their pre-erosion conditions, but the man-made buildings would have to be reconstructed from scratch by the survivors. A few animals were seen, giving hope that their populations would soon recover and that plentiful crops could once again grow from the land.

Normally, the king would have concentrated on rebuilding his kingdom *before* taking a bride. But as the royal heir was already on its way, wedding plans began immediately. And subsequently, so did the inquiries about his future bride. Reports flew about what happened at the castle that night to stop the curse. And none of them stood up to the truth. Once word got out that Ginny "the Troll Gurl" had been the one to save them, people crawled out of the woodwork to claim that the "orphan" was actually their daughter or sister, or they wanted to touch her, for magical healing or fertility properties.

Copious requests came in for Ginny, necessitating a need to designate a castle official to screen all requests. This boiled down to denying everyone admittance. The only family Ginny needed now was in Jeremie's chambers. This included Luke, who was always close by guarding them. He often kidded with her, saying things like, "If I had known you would turn out to be such a fox, I would have kissed you myself." It was a joke, of course. Luke had become like the brother she had never had.

Even the girls from the orphanage had come to see her. They were suspiciously sans Lydia, their prevailing leader and ever the opportunist. They declared to the guards that their acquaintance of Ginny made them "princesses by association." When Ginny heard they were still alive and waiting a few floors below, Jeremie and Luke both had to hold her back from going down there and killing them with her bare hands. Payback could be a bitch.

In the end, Ginny sent word that the girls should strip nakid and wait for her in preparation for a cleanliness and suitability inspection. She left them in a dark chamber for twelve hours, until one in the morning, before she had the guards dismiss them out of the castle forever.

They threw a lavish royal wedding. It was also a party in celebration of their survival. All the villagers were there, but the king and his new bride kept to a small inner circle. Luke kept out the curious ones who only wanted to gawk at the new-found beauty of the former troll gurl. She was still glowing, after all. It was like she carried a single torch's brightness with her everywhere she went. It got brighter if she was angry or upset. But it got brightest when she made love with Jeremie. On their wedding night it scared him. He feared his fate would become the same as the witch. It is a testament to how bright she was that someone who had been led to believe in magic all his life was still surprised at its impact. But he survived and learned to use it as a gauge of how much pleasure she was experiencing.

The fields were green again all across the land. What crops were still in them bloomed and bared fruit. But years of the curse had left many of them untilled and without seed. Those still surviving were to begin the process of bringing food to the kingdom again at once. They were even optimistic that with such a low population, they may be able to trade goods with outside lands again to help reacquire some of what they had lost. Trade had not happened in Jeremie and Ginny's lifetimes.

Many of the kingdom-folk also ended up working in the castle, just for the fact that there were not enough people to go around. Ginny had been raised to work, therefore she didn't mind cooking or cleaning. With such a shortage of manpower, even Jeremie found himself doing manual labor. It was a big adjustment for him, but it also gave him a greater appreciation for the hard work that went into the simplest things, such as food or clothing. If he caught her assisting in chores in her present gestating condition, Jeremie would stop her as soon as he caught her being productive. He wanted her to rest, to make sure this magic baby she carried could grow healthy within her womb.

As soon as the ingredients were available, he fed her all the decadent treats he had grown up with since birth that she had never tasted living on meager funds on the outskirts of the kingdom. She tried cakes and cookies and pastries. She tried frozen sweetened milk, which cooled her on a hot day. Her favorite may have been the cherry tarts that were glazed, then baked until crispy in the oven, and topped with a sprinkling of sugar dyed red. Once she tried these delights, Ginny never wanted regular food again. If you are what you eat, she wanted to have the sweetest baby possible.

In June, a baby boy was born. He glowed with the goodness that had saved the kingdom. And the royal family, small at it was, attempted to find some semblance of normal again.

Guinevere was in the sitting room, planning what to plant in the gardens for inside the castle courtyard come spring. The baby was napping. With it unusually quiet, she had become lost in her task and jumped when a knight entered from behind her.

"My Queen?"

Boy, was it weird to be referred to in that way.

"Yes, Luke?"

"There is another young lady here. Says she is your sister. She wants to hold council with you."

"Oh, God. Send her away, as you have all the other women from the orphanage. They think because I am married to the king now, I will grant them wealth and favor. I have not forgiven them for how they treated me as a girl. They can look at me now without revulsion. I cannot do the same for them."

"As you wish, Your Majesty."

With a small bow, Luke backed out the door of the room.

Minutes later, there was shouting outside the door. Scuffling against the stone floor became louder.

"No! You don't understand! I'm not from the orphanage. I'm her sister! Her flesh and blood sister! I want nothing from her but to know her. Tell her that. Tell her! Please!"

Hearing this, Guinevere jumped up and opened the door. In the hallway, struggling against two knights, with another quickly approaching, was a petite girl with blond hair and blue eyes. Guinevere did not recognize her from the orphanage. Maybe she had been a girl who had only stayed a short while. Maybe she was one of the lucky ones who had been taken in by a family to serve as a nanny or house girl.

"Guinevere? You don't know me. Well, you do. We used to play together as children. My grandmother lived near the orphanage. I'm Julie!"

"C'mon. Let's go," the newest knight grumbled as they began to haul her away.

"Julie?... Wait. Let her stay." Julie had been the only girl close to her own age that had ever been nice to her.

"Why have you come today, Julie?" Guinevere spoke to her with caution.

"Before my mother died of the plague, she told me a family secret. One I was not supposed to know, but one she could not carry with her to the grave."

"Go on."

"I always thought I was an only child. But then my mother confided in me that she disposed of her first born. That it had been a baby so ugly, she could not bear to put its face to her breast. She told the midwife to kill it, but later learned that the midwife had carried the baby to the orphanage."

"But I was told I was left on the doorstep with only a note."

"I don't know, but I don't think someone would lie about that. And you have to admit, we do look a little alike."

"We do...," Guinevere replied hesitantly. Guinevere could not really say. She was still not used to her new appearance, even though it had been a year. Often she thought she was someone else when she walked in front of a mirror.

Guinevere wanted to trust her. She wanted to believe that she could miraculously have some family out there in the land that would want to be a part of her life. All her days she had always been alone. How great would it be if all the parts of her life came together at once? A husband she loved, a baby, a brand new life... and a sister?

"Remember how mad my grandmother got when she caught us playing together? That is because *she knew*! She knew who you were. That is how the midwife knew about that orphanage, because my grandmother lived right next door. Grandmother told her where she could leave you."

There was a long silence as they both stared at each other. Guinevere wanted to believe this woman, but it would be too painful if it turned out to be untrue. All the knights had left except for Luke, who had been assigned by Jeremie to be Guinevere's personal bodyguard. He was never far away from her. The baby woke and began to cry. Guinevere instantly headed toward the nursery to retrieve him. Julie began to follow, but Luke blocked her way. This made Guinevere pause.

"Um, Luke, please take Julie into the dining room. Let the kitchen staff know to give her anything she wants to eat or drink. I need to consult with the king about this matter."

Luke nodded, and took Julie by the arm. This time she did not resist. He took her toward the dining room. Julie turned back to look at Guinevere again. It wasn't a look of celebrity, of fame. It was simply more genuine. They turned a corner and were out of sight.

Guinevere continued into the nursery and leaned into the crib, picking up the baby. Scooping him up, she bumped over the white teddy bear made of rabbit fur that perpetually sat guard in the corner of his crib. She held him against her, the babe instantly quieting at her touch. They had several nannies to help, but she felt it was important for the child to have a personal relationship with its father and mother, even if that is not how it was done for royalty in past generations. With the population decimated, they were quite open to new ideas. Everyone was just happy to still be alive, the king and new queen included.

She shook her head, trying to clear out the thoughts Julie had put in there. If only there was a way to confirm that the story was true. She left the nursery and headed to Jeremie's office, where there was a good chance he would be. As she passed the library, a possible solution came into her head.

She went in and surveyed the shelves for what she needed. The room was in disarray as she was in the process of moving much of it to a new location outside the castle that everyone could access. She wanted all the villagers to have a chance to learn to read and love books just as she had. She wanted to set up proper schools soon as well. The shelves were loaded with books and records, but not what she was looking for. Then she turned and began to riffle though the paperwork on the desks one handed, trying to balance the baby against her for more stability.

Then she found them. The records of the kingdom that Jeremie, herself, and the task force had compiled. She sat down, allowing her to more or less use both hands to flip through the pages of handwritten data as the baby lay against her chest. First she looked up the grandmother that had lived near the orphanage.

Evelyn O'Brien.

Could it be that old Mrs. O'Brien, who lived next door, had been Guinevere's grandmother all along? Had she watched her grow and simply ignored her? Could someone be that cruel?

Names had never been important to Guinevere. She had never had a last name. She had never known Miss Peters's first name. Her own first name had been shortened for most of her life. And there was the horrendous nickname that she still heard the children chant about her in her nightmares.

The cross-referenced records led her to the rest of the family in the next village over.

Daniel and Emily O'Brien.

Their daughter Julie.

The records indicated that Julie would have been seventeen at the time of the last sweep. Guinevere chuckled at the thought of Jeremie kissing his, well, seemed to be her sister. Of course there was no proof that these people had created her. Miss Peters kept no records. She had not even kept the note that had been in the basket with her.

But what if there had been no basket? Then there would not have been a note. What if it had been a midwife handing over a baby personally, and then hurrying away under the darkness of night before any questions about its appearance could be asked? Miss Peters had always assured her that she came from humans, and not trolls. This would explain her confidence in that assumption. And it was not that far out of the realm of possibility that new parents would have been frightened of their new child. It hurt her heart, that was for sure, but she could understand it. And it could have been worse. They could have drowned her in the well and buried her in a shallow grave, and no one would have known the difference. It was a miracle that she had lived long enough for the curse to be broken. She herself had wanted to end her own life on many occasions, never realizing its value.

The records proved these people were indeed who Julie claimed they were. Guinevere would have to take a leap of faith if she was going to trust Julie. She let herself shed a few tears. She gathered up the baby, and headed to the dining room.

Julie was seated at the table, drinking a goblet of wine. In front of her were a chicken, a plate of steamed vegetables, and another plate filled with desserts, untouched. Julie jumped up when she saw Guinevere.

"Oh, you are back! Oh my gosh," she covered her mouth. "Is that the new prince?"

"Yes."

"Can I hold him?" She approached Guinevere. Guinevere waved off Luke, who made a move to block Julie.

"I would like to ask you something else, first."

"Sure, of course. Anything." Julie had already begun to raise her arms in preparation of taking the child, but as Guinevere was obviously not going to give him up yet, Julie simply waved her arms at her sides instead.

"What do you want?"

"What do I want?" Julie repeated.

"It was nice seeing you today. But what do you expect tomorrow? Or next week? Or for Winter Holiday?" She tried to be kind, but serious.

"With our mother and father gone now, I have no other family. I want to get to know you. I thought you might want to know me or at least what has become of me since we played in the woods as kids. I was hoping we could have a relationship, I guess."

"You must realize that you are not the first person from my past to come knocking on the castle doors. I turned them all away without a second thought. You must understand the position I am in as queen. I can't risk harm coming to my husband, my child, or the kingdom. I have verified that your family is who you say they are. But there are no records of my birth. I have nothing to go on but my gut instinct and our shared eye color."

"I understand. I can go and never return if that is your decision," Julie replied.

"I have another question for you."

"Anything."

"You aren't an evil witch pretending to be my sister, are you?"

"What?" Julie asked, perplexed.

"I had to check." Guinevere shook her head. "Please, come meet your nephew, Kellin."

"Oh, God. Thank you," Julie gushed.

Guinevere handed over the new prince as Luke grumbled in disapproval in the corner.

"I can offer you some assistance in these times of rebuilding from the king's standard loss of person and property fund, of course. But any further contact and reunion will have to be earned over time. I am sorry it has to be this way."

"No, no. When you explain it like that, I totally understand... Hello, big boy," Julie cooed at him as she lifted his body up and down, his chubby legs dangling beneath him. He made happy baby noises as she played with him.

"What they say about him is true."

"What is that?" Guinevere asked.

"That he has a healthy glow about him."

"Oh, that. A lingering side effect of the curse. It doesn't cause him any malady. We have all grown used to it."

"My, um, our grandmother would tell me that Miss Peters was a responsible woman who took care of her duties. I never thought that sounded like a fun woman to be around. "

"Oh, she wasn't. But she took care of all of us when no one else would. It takes a huge heart to do that."

"Grandmother said that Miss Peters had been madly in love once, when she was young. A peddler came through and stole her heart, but her parents said he wasn't good enough for her and they wouldn't pay her dowry. Grandmother said it broke her heart and she never recovered. That is why she only gave herself to serving godly pursuits after that."

"Wow. I never knew. I can't imagine her ever being young. That story would explain some mysteries of her personality when she was older. And about how she never forgave me for making a purchase from a peddler when I was younger."

Guinevere smiled at how easily Julie took to the baby, and he to her. It warmed her heart. She could swear that her precious baby boy began to glow even brighter.

hat? You just let her into our lives? Without even consulting me? Whose castle is this, anyway?"

"Yours. Everyone knows who owns the castle and how big it is," Ginny retorted. Jeremie snickered at her disapprovingly as he paced the stone floor in his office. "And I didn't let her into our lives. I met with her and gave her her share of the hardship fund. I thought that was within my wifely duties."

"It is," he wrung his hands, frustrated with her. "But you let her see our son. Hold him!"

"Who told you that?" she asked indignantly.

"Luke. Why? Would you have kept it from me?"

"Possibly. But he was there, protecting us both, in case she was a potential crazy. Which, for the record, I do not think that she is.

"Look, you don't know, alright?" Ginny went on. "What it feels like to not have anyone to count on, to tuck you in to a safe bed at night, to have to constantly look over your shoulder. You and Kellin are a great family. And Luke—"

"Luke?" he barked, confused.

"I think of him as a brother-in-law."

"Oh, I guess I could see that," he grimaced.

"But the thought that I could have other family out there or an actual blood relative... it is almost too good to believe."

"You made my point for me. It *is* too good to believe. The rumor mill is well acquainted with your life story. That is why we have con artists knocking on our door every day. Baby, I get that you want this to be the real deal, but there is a good chance that there isn't any family left for you out there."

Ginny was quiet for a few moments as she contemplated his words. She went to stand by the window, looking out at the black mountains, her back to Jeremie. A group of children were playing below, jumping rope. Their chant rose up to meet her from where she watched several floor up:

I see roses
I jump with my feet
All that is true
Can't be beat
I see the king
I see the queen
Up in the tower
so high, high
Don't let them die
Don't let her fall
She is the one who saved us all.

"It's Julie," she informed him.

"What? Who's Julie?"

"Julie. Remember when I told you about the only friend I had as a girl?"

"That was Julie?" he paused, considering. "It's been years. How can you even be sure it is her?"

Ginny turned back around to face him.

"Because I never told anyone about her, except you. She knew about our time together. My gut says she is the real deal."

"Well, if your heart says so. How can I argue with that?" he smiled.

"Thank you. I'll go slow, I promise."

"And her visits are *always* monitored... by Luke."

"Yes master." She wrapped her arms around his waist. She kissed him, enjoying that their heights were now more compatible.

"Hey. That's 'Your Majesty' to you." He squeezed her tightly, constricting her painful past right out of her.

# EPILOGUE

A woman's scream echoed through the cold, stone castle hallways. Guinevere was awakened from her slumber, but didn't realize what had roused her. Instead, her first thoughts strayed to how she sometimes missed the natural warmth of the bedhouse, with its seasoned wood walls and thatch roof at the orphanage where she grew up. It had been a nice place on the rare occasions that she was in it alone. The castle was cold, drab stone everywhere you looked. But it was built that way for a reason, having held up to the destroying forces of the curse just long enough for her and the king to find a way to stop it. The bunkhouse didn't last more than a few decades.

A second scream rang out, and the sound of several guards jogging by outside the door to her chamber made her sit up. She turned to find Jeremie's side of the bed empty; he was already up. Guinevere threw on her heavy robe to protect against the chill and ran to the door. Once in the hallway, she was met with the sight of Lucy, the morning nanny, crying in front of her son's nursery door, surrounded by the guards. Guinevere did not let her thoughts reach their logical conclusion. She ran as fast as she could past the two rooms in between. She pushed the knights aside to enter the room. They parted for her easily.

All she found there was an empty crib.

Her breath immediately escaped her lungs. She turned to look at the guards and the nanny for an explanation. No tears came out of her eyes, only pure shock and terror.

"Luke came to my quarters and said there had been some sort of break in to the castle last night. He said I should check the baby right away. I came right down, but he, but he…"

"…was gone," Guinevere finished, falling to her knees. One of the knights rushed to her side. She didn't know which one. It didn't matter. It was not her friend Luke, who would have brought some small amount of solace to this situation. "Where is Jeremie now?"

"The king is with Luke," the knight holding her answered. "Last time I saw them, they were at the gate."

"Get him now, please."

"He has already been sent for," another in the doorway responded.

No sooner had the words escaped his lips, but more footfalls could be heard approaching.

"No, no. It cannot be," Jeremie said, as he ran to the doorway, finding the only family member in the room to be his wife. "Is it true? They have taken Kellin?"

"Yes," Guinevere sobbed, as she fell from the guard into her husband's arms.

"We allowed security to become too lax. Luke, immediately send out a search party of knights down every road. Have the servants canvass those in the shadow of the castle to find out if they saw *anything*." He turned to Guinevere. "We *will* find him."

And just like that, their happily ever after was stolen from them, much like a beautiful, enchanted baby boy.

## EMBRACE YOUR WEIRDNESS
## LOVE YOURSELF

**JENNIFER FRIESS** is an author, blogger, and editor who lives in Lenawee County, Michigan, with her husband, son, and dog. She loves entertainment trivia. She doesn't match her socks. She is a picky eater and likes it that way. Jennifer is the author of The Riley Sisters series, available now in paperback or on your favorite device.

Follow Jennifer here:

**BLOG:** ImNotStalkingYou.com
My mildly entertaining random thoughts

**TWITTER:** @jenf2

**FACEBOOK:** www.facebook.com/imnotstalkingyou2